THE CULTIVATION OF WEEDS

Emory Menefee

ExPress

El Cerrito, California

This novel is entirely fictional, with no intent
to depict actual persons or events other than
those within a few historical allusions

Published by ExPress,
P.O. Box 1639, El Cerrito, CA 94805
expresspublishing.com

Distributed by National Book Network
4501 Forbes Boulevard, Lanham, MD 20706

ISBN: 978-0-932956-31-6
Library of Congress Control Number: 2007936954

Printed in the U.S.A.
Data Reproductions Corp.

THE CULTIVATION OF WEEDS

FOR JO

Chapter 1
Carl

On a forest trail in midsummer, sunlight streaming down through the trees can sometimes produce a striking mosaic of light and shadow on the pathway. Patterns like this were important to the impressionist masters, and their paintings of them remind us that such blotches of light and shade are as complementary as pollen and bee. In the quiet woods, the effect distills our mood into one of contemplation and encourages us to enjoy the lethargy of summer.

Carl Grendil often walked along a path like this in parkland not far from where he lived. The images of shade and light had a strangely powerful fascination for him, almost an addiction, and he felt enlivened when the weather and season collaborated to produce unusually pleasing patterns. He often photographed them for later study to try to learn why some shots worked and others didn't. Though the photos became a comforting map for the territory, he knew they were merely abstractions that could always be improved on. He had taught himself the principles of photographic composition and processing well enough that his work was admired within the family and the very few others who saw it, though hardly anyone ever asked him for a print.

Sadly, Carl's favorite walks amid the impressionist shadows were losing their appeal to him. Many of the wooded areas adjacent to the park were under development for new housing, not on a large scale, but steadily. Carl could hear the sounds of workmen, and while the pleasure of his walks was not yet lost, he feared the worst. He took photos more often, and cherished them more than ever.

Several decades before, Carl's father purchased the family home from a workman who had lost his job and was obliged to leave to find work elsewhere. This man had built the house himself and in spite of some eccentricities it offered a strongly comforting space to grow up in and to feel separate from the world outside. Carl was born there, the only home he had known. It was on a lot large enough to make it invisible to neighbors and passersby, which suited Carl's reclusive habits perfectly. The sylvan setting seemed entirely safe to his parents, and they allowed him to roam freely at any time.

After the local industry failed, the town of Woodville lay unnoticed by real estate agents and developers for years, until its recent rediscovery as a preferred place to live. It turned out to be an ideal refuge for the affluent of the city who were seeking to escape the restive homeless hordes and rampant crime that had affected urban areas all over the country in the wake of the worst economic slump the country had yet suffered. Woodville was far enough from the city to retain its country setting but close enough for those who had reasons to go there. As magazine ads brought buyers, trees were cut and new roads built. Carl noticed a steady rise in the number of hikers and dog owners exercising their pets. He tried to find times for his walks when the outsiders didn't come so often, but the compulsive fascination of the paths began to fade. A mood of apathy grew on him, and he retreated more and more to his room and the company of his photographs. He still walked, but into entirely different places, and without the enthusiasm he once felt. Eventually, however, and to his surprise, he found on one of these walks an agreeable substitute for his park trails.

The old industrial zone of Woodville was located not far from Carl's house, in a direction opposite to that of the parkland. It was ringed by a rusting railway, narrow gauge tracks that seemed to form a kind of frame surrounding the abandoned factories that had sprung up some 50 years earlier. This was the industry that had created the town and brought in a few hundred workers who settled in the hilly woods nearby. After the tracks were built, the railroad gave the town its name of Woodville, uninspired but accurate enough. It thrived for about a generation, with newcomers arriving in a steady stream and building houses close to the works, like the one now owned by the Grendils. As often happens with small and isolated industrial centers like Woodville, the methods of production changed, shipping became cheaper from more central yards, and overseas labor took over, so the factories gradually moved away or closed altogether. Most of the buildings were simply abandoned, some chained and locked carefully by their owners who halfheartedly hoped that one day a revival of the industry would make them salable, a vain hope after the entire economy failed. Many buildings were left open and uncared for, to decay and crumble from wind and water. A few of the smallest businesses struggled to hang on for a while, but for the most part it became an industrial graveyard. The revival never happened, and the new urban escapees in their upscale houses looked on the buildings as a blight. There was talk about razing them and making a mall, but all the proposals had died for lack of funding or, more likely, for lack of enough potential users to make such an idea profitable. The buildings were mostly left untended.

Carl had known of the decaying industrial park all his life and was aware of its quiet desolation, though as a disinterested onlooker rather than a participant. He called it the "Zone." With his beloved park walks losing their appeal, he began to realize that the streets and alleys of this skeletal relic could also offer a stimulating place to walk alone and savor light and shadow. With the eye of a photographer, he found that the geometry of street and building in the Zone could create fascinating images of sun and darkness with the serenity he had known in the parklands, though now the serenity would come from desolation and emptiness rather than the calm of the forest. In this seemingly unlikely setting, he found that he could recover a comforting dreamy and superreal imagery when walking among the buildings and around the abandoned railroad station with its peeling "Woodville" sign. Cracked walkways with small tufts of weeds became focal points on the sunlit streets and walkways, made more vivid by the blackness of shadows along the base of the walls and on bits of abandoned equipment left to rust. While the quietness of a forest setting is natural and detached from the human world, the quietness of an abandoned architecture arouses an awareness of people long gone. Carl found that his obsession was indeed transferable.

On nearly any sunny day Carl would walk slowly along the streets of the Zone, savoring the melancholy mood of the light around aging brick and concrete structures that showed the decay of age and neglect. He especially liked the crumbling copies of formal devices over arched doors and windows, remnants of an effort to impose a vaguely classical look on the architecture. Usually, after he had studied a scene for a long time, he would take a photograph of it with the small camera he always carried with him. He brought a bottle of water that he often shared with some of the tiny weeds in the cracks of the pavement, tying up in some way his life with theirs.

Carl Grendil was twenty three years old, with time on his hands. He had never trained for any kind of vocation, nor worked at any regular job. For a while he attended a small private college named Forburn and located not far from Woodville. He mostly enrolled in what interested him, especially the history of science, but he never finished enough of the college's requirements to get a degree, even though his professors had considered him an above average student. Even had he finished, however, his record would not likely arouse much interest among personnel directors.

He was tall and slender with light brown hair and a squarish face, with an angular jaw that gave him a severe and somewhat military look. His intense and piercing eyes actively reflected a keen interest in observing whatever went on around him. He kept himself in good physical condition, not because of any personal goal, but simply because he walked a lot and had little interest in food other than as a necessity. He dressed simply and had acquired a wardrobe consisting of identical pants, shirts, shoes and socks, so that he wasted no time in outfitting himself for the day.

He liked living with his parents in their old and comfortable house, which was large enough that days could pass without his seeing them, though he didn't especially try to avoid them. They had become accustomed to having a son who had no interest in leaving each morning to work, and they could afford to indulge his idleness. His daily walks, often ten miles or more, kept him away from the house much of the day, and usually his meals were taken whenever he felt hungry, from whatever leftovers were in the refrigerator. He had an easygoing and placid personality, with a way of talking that made others feel comfortable. Even so, he rarely smiled or indicated any facial emotion at all, though he relished an amusing story and could shed a tear at a sad one.

He adjusted easily to a new routine in the Zone, and rarely returned to the tree lined pathways in the park. He would walk among the deserted buildings almost every day, barring dangerously stormy conditions. During merely inclement weather his fascination with light and shadow gave way to observing the melancholia of the deserted streets. Days, weeks, and months went by like this, until a special day came that was quite different from all those before. He had left the house fairly early, as usual, and arrived at the industrial area after a short walk, at a time when the sun had begun casting long geometric shadows along the streets. As it brightened, he felt its reassuring warmth, feeling secure in the constancy of his limited world, believing that by indulging his visual obsession with light he could feel a palpable sense that all was right.

He rarely met anyone in these streets. If he did, it would be someone he had seen before, most likely a former owner of one of the buildings wistfully looking at a lost investment. He never felt that he was being watched by anyone else, nor did the thought occur to him. But on this morning he noticed in the distance, moving in and out of view around the standing ruins, the figure of a girl, someone he couldn't recognize.

Her walk, with its careless abandon, seemed almost like a kind of personal dance, as though she were responding to music unheard by anyone else. Her movements were not so much a walk as a random motion, though it gradually brought her closer to him. As she neared, he saw that she was young, probably about his age, with a pleasing appearance in spite of hair that was a little stringy and a prominent nose and jaw that made her look almost masculine. She was not tall, but her slenderness and vivacity gave her a peculiarly regal appearance, so that while many would not find her beautiful, Carl was impressed.

He usually felt that his privacy was being invaded whenever he saw anyone else in the Zone. But something was different about this young woman. He couldn't tell yet because she was too far away, but as he watched her, more and more fascinated, the surroundings seemed, in his imagination at least, to be transformed from the dark and light contrasts of a crumbling industrial area to hot and roofless stone ruins in some ancient country, high columns holding huge lintels outside walls of great limestone blocks etched by centuries of weather. The woman too had become classical in some way, her simple dress taking on a timeless look, and her very visage a classic profile. He began to feel he had seen her before.

She eventually made her way to him, and he saw that she carried a small notebook. She handed it to him and he read an account of walks among the ruins and desolate paths that was strangely similar to how he would have described them. He thought she must have been there with him, watching him.

She closed the book and walked a short distance to where an old rusting pipe jutted horizontally from the side of a building. She straddled it as she kept her eyes on him. The contrast of her white thighs against the rust color of the pipe excited him, and though he was inexperienced in such matters, he felt heated, attracted, and confused, all at once. She seemed a complete stranger to him, and yet somehow he thought he had known her before. He had never even come close to having a sexual relationship with a woman, nor for that matter attempted to make more than superficial contact with women he had known in high school or college. But before he had time to reflect and put his feelings into context – after all, he had merely encountered an attractive woman as she walked along a deserted street – she jumped from the pipe and ran toward him. In a voice slightly hoarse and low-pitched she said, "I'm Mora. Don't you remember seeing me before?"

"No," he replied, "I don't recall. I'm not sure. You do look familiar in a way, but I don't know why. I guess I've been preoccupied."

"Yes, I know that. I've watched you for quite a while. I know that you are Carl Grendil. We were in school together, but I suppose you don't remember me from there. You never seemed interested in girls in those days."

He guessed she knew about his obsession with light patterns, and felt a little foolish at having it being known by anyone else. He couldn't think of anything interesting to say, anything that would impress her. He blurted out, "Why would you be interested in me? Are you some kind of a stalker?" He knew it was a stupid remark as soon as he said it. He had no idea how stalkers operated, or why he would say such a thing, other than that he had heard about them on the newscasts.

"I go after what pleases me, and I like what little I know about you," she said. Her tone was provocative and suggestive. "I was really impressed with you in school. You seemed to understand everything so easily. I'd like to have gotten to know you then, but I guess maybe I was a little shy myself. I always thought we might have been friends, maybe even a lot alike. I wasn't stalking you now, just trying to learn a little more about you. I didn't mean to make you nervous."

"I'm not really nervous. It's just that I don't know much about how to talk to women."

"I'll teach you. Let's go for a coffee."

This was more an order than a proposal. He agreed, and they left the Zone to enter a small café not far away, the Angelou, one of the few lingering businesses struggling to survive. They sat by a window and got their coffee, a thick brew that had been left heating for hours.

"Not great, but at least it's hot," she said.

"I don't really drink coffee much. It seems ok to me."

They sat with only occasional talking for what seemed to him an uncomfortably long time. Their attempts at finding common threads fizzled. Finally she asked, "Would you come with me for an outing tomorrow? I'd like to show you something."

He had no idea of what to say. "Well, I don't know. This whole thing of meeting up with you seems really strange to me. I'm not actually worried, but it's just kind of strange."

"Don't worry. I'll be there with a friend, just to make you more comfortable. What if I come by around 10 in the morning, near where we met today? I'll be in a dark car, with a driver. I don't feel comfortable about driving. Is it a date?"

Carl sat quietly for a while, trying to think of what might happen to him. She seemed like a normal young woman, as far as he could tell. Still, his thoughts flitted to a movie he had once seen, in which a woman seduced a guy to go to a remote place outside town for some wild sex, or so he thought. Instead, he was beaten and robbed by a couple of beefy thugs in armless tee shirts. Nevertheless, Carl could not feel much threat in the advances Mora had made toward him. After all, people do have to meet somehow, even in strange ways like this.

"Ok, I'll go."

"I know it seems brash of me, asking you like this, but I just know you haven't had that much experience in dating women. It's pretty normal for women to ask men out nowadays. Most men really like it. It's nearly always hard for guys to make the first move."

"I'm not worried." He tried to smile. "I'll be here. I usually am."

Mora smiled genuinely, and went out of the café. A car was waiting for her, with a driver, as she had said.

Carl walked back to the place they had met, and stayed there for a time, sitting on a block of limestone. The sun was getting low, and the shadows were long and dark. He started home.

His parents Ed and Lyn were sitting on the porch when he walked up. Ed was reading something, and didn't look up, though he did, and sharply, when Carl announced, "You'll never guess. I've got a date for tomorrow."

"Oh, that's exciting," Lyn said. "Your first one, I think. How did you meet?" She tried to make her voice belie the doubt she had that Carl would ever find anyone with whom to share his life.

Carl gave a brief account that intentionally made his meeting with Mora seem more normal than what actually happened. He implied that he asked her to have coffee and then made a date.

Ed glanced up at him, "When I was your age, I was married. It didn't last, but I was married."

"Well, I'm not. Things just don't happen that way with me." Carl went inside. He didn't want to have to explain anything else about Mora just yet.

Ed looked at Lyn before settling back to his reading. "It worked," he said. "I just hope it's the best thing for Carl. I talked a few weeks ago with Bob Smith, an agent I know from the Division of Intelligence, not his real name, of course. I don't think you know him. He gave me some ideas about an organization that might be good for Carl, and that's how it got started. He arranged for the girl to meet him. She's a kind of recruiter. We'll have to see what develops."

Lyn didn't seem concerned. At this point it was enough for her that Carl would actually be having a date.

Chapter 2
Family

Ed Grendil stood on the porch and watched a blimp slowly glide overhead, the second time it had passed by that day. It had the lettering MEGALIFE on the side.

"Son of a bitch. Son of a bitch." Ed's voice got louder with each word. "If I had a big enough gun, I'd bring that thing down." He was yelling. Lyn came to the door.

"Come on, Ed, it doesn't do any good to get mad."

"Get mad? How can you not get mad? The insurance companies are near the top of the list of things that have ruined this country. They are just a bunch of greedy, vicious criminals trying to bilk people when they're most vulnerable."

She mustered a small laugh, "Well, I don't know. We were paid off pretty quickly when you totaled the car."

"That's a shoo-in for them. They know the statistics inside out, and know damn well they are going to end up with a big profit even when they do have to pay off. I'm talking about the huge catastrophes of life. You have your house blown away by a tornado, wrecked by an earthquake, or washed away in a flood, not to speak of personally coming down with cancer or a stroke. The insurance companies work overtime to try to avoid paying off. It's like a two-bit gambler trying to weasel out of a bet. And that's if you have insurance. If you don't have any insurance at all, well, you're completely shit out of luck. But even if you have enough money to try to buy a policy and they think you've got some health problem, you won't get any insurance at all. You can only get it if they're convinced that you won't need it."

"It's always been done by insurance companies," Lyn said. "I don't know who else would take care of unforeseen problems. If it weren't for them there would be nothing."

"That's the whole point. Here we are in the richest country ever, and we don't even look after each other. How hard would it be to have a national fund to take care of people in trouble? Sure, there has to be oversight to make sure the bad apples don't abuse the system. Some kind of effective public control, not just some autonomous agency with career bureaucrats to administer the funds. We've got a lot of smart and honest people up and down the ladder. It will work if we want it to, and my guess is that almost everyone in the country wants it to."

"But, Ed, you don't like the bureaucracy we already have. I don't see how this would be that much different."

"It is different. Like I just said, of course you have to have an agency of some kind with authority and tools to act in emergencies, but it should be controlled by citizens empowered to make decisions and get rid of anyone who doesn't play honestly. A real democracy, from people who would be affected by loss, not by a tiny group of wealthy executives and vested politicians."

Lyn was sorry she had encouraged him. His voice had taken on the sharp and slightly high pitched tones that indicated he was ranting. He went on, "It would pay off without a hassle whenever a citizen is hit by a catastrophe. Private insurance, it's a joke. Look at health care. Privately run, managed by insurance, everybody with a hand has it in the pot, from doctors and drug companies to the guy building a hospital room. What kind of madness would support a system where the people who collect the premiums and stand to profit are the ones who not only decide who is eligible but how much they should be paid, or even if they get paid anything at all?"

She went into the kitchen to make a couple of cool drinks, and brought them out. Ed pushed himself back on the chaise, took the drink and calmed down. "You know, Lyn, the politicos know about the problems. They have seen the movies on global warming, health care, and all that, but nothing ever happens."

Ed Grendil was fifty plus, balding and overweight by a few pounds. He looked a little like Senator McCarthy from the

1950s, though his ideas could not be more different. He often seemed hyperactive, ready to jump up and immediately get involved in something that interested or disturbed him. When he had taught physics at Forburn, his students were awed and intimidated by him as he strode back and forth across the front of the classroom, shouting out something he thought would be important for them to know. Perhaps because of his temperament, he was casually acquainted with many people but had no close friends he could confide in. His wife was his best friend.

Lyn was barely forty but looked about half that. A tanned brunette, trim and fit, she projected the very image of calmness, a successful result of hiding her stress. She released her nervous energy by physically working out rather than by hyperventilating the way Ed did. They had lived in their Woodville house since they were married and had raised all three of their children there. Carl was first, followed in a couple of years by the twins, Max and Anna. Of all the children, Anna seemed to be the brightest and most self motivated. She diligently studied music and became a proficient pianist. Max did a little drawing, but it suffered from his chronic depression that persisted in spite of treatment by the usual battery of antidepressant drugs. He spent much of his time by himself, though whenever Anna was receptive he would attach himself to her. He regarded her almost reverently because of her accomplishments and self confidence. The three siblings became inseparable playmates and friends,

all the more important to them during those years when Ed
and Lyn saw only occasional visitors for the oddly formal
events they staged to celebrate birthdays or other milestones.
Perhaps in an effort to compensate, the parents gave their
children nearly every kind of interactive toy and game that
they could find, from Monopoly to state-of-the-art computer
and video games. On cold or rainy days, the three children
would always be together, sometimes playing, sometimes
reading to each other, sometimes feigning to argue about some
current event that Ed had brought up for them to debate. In
good weather, they would play on the tennis court Ed had
built, his one concession to extravagance. Anna had some
serious aspirations toward making something of herself,
perhaps in music, but Carl and Max were merely content to
think of those moments when the three were together as being
all they needed from life.

In their teens, Carl and Max became more and more
withdrawn, insisting on their solitude as though it were a right.
Lyn sometimes thought she had failed somehow as a mother.
Still, she could at least carry on a conversation with Carl,
though he seemed more reserved with her than even with
complete strangers who came to the house. Max took the
solitariness of Carl a step further, almost to hermitism. Aside
from doing a little outdoor painting that revealed only a
mediocre talent, he usually sat alone in his room, unwilling to
participate in what the family as a whole was doing. Whenever
possible, he ate alone, and rarely spoke to Lyn or to Ed. His

attachment to Anna persisted, perhaps because he felt some special bonding that came from their being twins. Ed and Lyn provided him with the best counseling they could find in the Woodville area, but his attachment to solitude persisted. He seemed to revel in isolation, and eventually ended up communicating almost only to Anna.

Unexpectedly, both Max and Anna left home when they were eighteen, to Lyn's great disappointment. Lyn most of all missed Anna, with whom she had developed a strong bond, entirely unlike her relationship with the reclusive Max. Carl was also deeply disturbed by their departure. His own lesser detachment from social intercourse had come to seem almost normal by having Anna and Max around, both of whom showed little or no interest in developing their social skills. He was most comfortable with Anna, who seemed to be more conventional, and he spent as much time with her as he could. When he confided in her, he knew he very likely could never attain that kind of agreeable rapport with anyone else.

Primarily for lack of anything better to do with himself, Carl stayed after the twins left home. He never tried to develop any other close friendships. Ed Grendil sometimes wondered whether Carl had some kind of mental illness, and had him visit a therapist when he was about fifteen years old. The sessions revealed nothing extraordinary so Ed insisted they be stopped after a short time, even though Carl liked the relaxed conversations he had with the psychologist. His principal family involvement was providing simple company for Lyn when Ed was away on a "personal excursion" or occasionally conferring with his partner Robert Sikes. Sometimes Lyn would try to act like a friend to Carl, the way Anna and Max had, but the effort always seemed doomed to fail. She felt his isolation as keenly as she felt her own after the twins left home, and would have loved to find a way to bring him out of his loneliness, for her own selfish needs for companionship as much as anything else. Her loneliness grew more profound year after year.

By nearly any standard, Lyn's beauty would be remarkable, not merely because of her striking appearance, but more subtly in the way she projected herself with an air of mystery and invitation. Her dark flowing hair, which she admitted to tinting now and then, seemed always to land on her shoulders in the most provocative way. She knew the powerful effect she had on the men she ran into, and consciously kept this power coiled like a snake for whenever it may be useful to her. She had been just nineteen when she became pregnant with Carl, and now even at forty and having had three children, she looked much the same. In earlier years she and Ed reveled in acting out wild sexual games, and now, much later, she often still lived in a fantasized world of eroticism. Whether for reasons of her age, or, as she suspected, from his having other relationships, Ed had lost interest in her games. On rare occasions he enjoyed trying to act the animal again, but he had recently become more lamb than lion. Their moments of intimacy were rare.

For some years Ed had taught physics at Forburn College, a small private school conveniently close to home. He earned a barely livable salary, but since the teaching assignments were not time consuming, he had plenty of time and energy for his own research projects, at least as long as they required no outside funding. They were carried out in a small outbuilding behind the house. He called it his research laboratory, and going to it made him think of himself as a scientist. He was average in his understanding of physical theory, but he did understand how things work, and how to design them to make them work.

Twenty years before he'd had the idea for a spy chip that ended up making him rich. He didn't know how to produce and manufacture the actual chip, but he was able to find a partner who did, a reputedly brilliant physicist skilled in nanotechnology and computer fundamentals whom he had met at a seminar at Berkeley.

Robert Sikes was ten years younger than Ed, about Lyn's age. He had a difficult and contentious personality that caused him to take consulting work and temporary assignments rather than try to hold conventional jobs, from which he had been fired several times. He had managed to get his PhD in physics from Berkeley, though he had found himself often in stormy confrontation with his professors and thesis advisor. After studying computer science, he decided to go into that field and as a consultant found himself extremely successful in designing chips for specialized computer applications. He knew, or knew of, almost everything involving chips and computers. Many of his associates felt he had serious mental problems, and though he didn't seem violent, they avoided him whenever possible. Ed Grendil felt the same way about Sikes, but he felt bound to him because of the extraordinary brilliance that he brought to turning rough theory into reality.

The chip idea that Ed had come up with and which Robert developed was actually quite simple. When large computers were sold to other countries, or to anyone for that matter, the F-chip, as it was called, could be installed to sample whatever went through the main bus of the processor. It was designed to transmit a Fourier transform of all this information, with enough power to be picked up by a satellite antenna overhead. Once the transform was deconvoluted, the receiver had access to all the information processed by the computer. Anyone else picking up the signal from the chip, anywhere in its vicinity, would hear what would sound like weak white noise. If the chip were removed or tampered with, the Fourier circuit would self destruct and revert to one that merely passed data through unchanged. The computer would then operate as usual, with or without the chip. To be even more undetectable, the transform had been altered; the chance of having their secret blown was nearly zero.

When Ed Grendil and Robert Sikes showed the chip to the U.S. Division of Intelligence, their technical staff knew instantly what it would do for them. They immediately put Ed and Robert under the highest security, and forbade them to make any mention of the chip to anyone, much less try to patent it or sell it. The DI let them know that any breach of secrecy would bring dire and instant retaliation and even hinted at possible death. The F-chip was put into computers that ended up in all the major government offices of the world and quickly became a pipeline for secret information funneled directly to the DI. Privately, Ed and Robert were showered with money for their part in the chip development, though they were frequently warned about what would happen to them if one word of it got out. Ed was greatly put off by this, partly because he felt that publication of a paper on the F-chip would be his best chance for scientific recognition, and partly because he disliked bureaucratic kneejerk control. But after it got into the hands of the DI, it was too late.

Robert Sikes seemed content just to take the money and let the government decide how the chip should be used. The whole F-chip idea became one of the tightest-kept secrets in the history of the country. For years it gave Washington deep insight into the affairs of governments all over the world. Even after the Internet and satellites came to dominate information transfer, the chip still found frequent use, though by then other methods for data tapping were being developed.

Still, Ed and Robert never had any further concern about their financial security. They had enough banked to last for life, and even Ed became adjusted to the strictures of maintaining total secrecy.

Lyn Grendil never had any idea what her husband did to earn so much money. He told her and a few inquisitive friends that he and Robert had come up with some popular improvements in chip design that were of value to computer manufacturers and game developers. As far as giving away the actual purpose of the chip to Lyn, he knew that she also would be marked for retaliation if the leak became known. Carl, Max, and Anna were even more in the dark. They were happy to keep it that way and never showed the slightest interest in how Ed earned his living. Max and Anna each got an allowance check every month, and Ed never asked what they did with it.

When they left home, Anna and Max moved to a small northern town, where Anna taught music almost for free to low income families, while Max dabbled with painting, spending days at a time on unfinished projects in his studio. They felt they had to escape the life sucking structure of the Grendil household, but neither of them had any kind of plan for the future.

Carl remained in Woodville, staying at home in the same room he had occupied since childhood, hoping somehow that a chance event might change his life and open the world to him. His needs were few, so it was no strain for Ed and Lyn to give him whatever he wanted. He had developed an early interest in photography, and this had become the one thing that he felt he could do well. His studies in light and shadow had become to him more than just important but almost obsessive. It was the only thing he did that gave any structure to his life, justifying his long hours spent in studying the pathways of the forest and now the dilapidated structures in the Zone.

So, in these ways time passed at the Grendil home. Everyone in the family was ready for some great change in their lives, though nobody yet knew how it might happen.

Chapter 3
The meeting

During the night, Carl thought a lot about his coming date, or meeting, or whatever it might best be called. Until Mora appeared, almost like an intruder into his life, he hadn't thought much about relationships at all. During his years in public school, and even into college, he was almost entirely a loner with a reputation for being weird. Some thought he might be homosexual, an orientation considered to be a perversion in those days, and they often whispered among themselves the glib sexual innuendos current among teens. Almost nobody talked to him in a friendly way, and even in his early grades, when girls were usually more trusting and open, they barely saw him as a person. It didn't matter to him. He enjoyed doing the exercises in class, the homework, and especially gaining a glow of accomplishment whenever he turned in a completed assignment.

Mora's abrupt entry into his life made him realize how lonely he really was, and that maybe he did need human involvement, some warmth beyond the occasional family discussions at home. Part of it could be the sexual desire that he'd felt for years but had never allowed to become a dominant part of his thought. As he had discovered when he was quite young, there was an easy way to physically satisfy his erotic feelings and temporarily dispel the sexual images that intruded on his thoughts. But his feelings right now were different.

The idea that someone was out there who actually wanted to get acquainted with him was a new one, and he liked it, though he wondered why anyone like Mora, so outgoing, would have the slightest interest in him. The way he and Mora had met still unnerved him, but he thought the outing with her today would smooth all that out, and maybe answer his questions.

He dressed in his standard outfit, khaki pants, a long sleeved tan shirt, and hiking shoes, part of the everyday wardrobe he had designed to avoid having to make choices. He usually took along a nondescript grayish jacket, even when the day was mild. As he pulled on his shoes, he thought about whether he may need something more dressy if he and Mora actually went somewhere besides the dingy local café. But all that could be sorted out later.

When Carl had his morning coffee in the kitchen, Ed and Lyn had already gone out for the day – Ed to his laboratory and Lyn out to meet friends. He was glad he didn't have to explain any more to them than he already had. There would be plenty of time for details when he came back that evening. He would have to tell them something about how he spent the day, but he knew they wouldn't ask any difficult questions. He thought they had most likely given up on his ever finding a girlfriend, much less getting married and settling down as a husband, and he himself had come to think the same thing. He couldn't predict anything about his relationship with

Mora, but he felt something might happen between them. Right now this something was merely a sexual tingling, the sort of thing that usually starts happening to boys at least ten years younger.

He left the house to walk toward the Zone. It was much too early, but he didn't care. He could easily spend the time in his usual preoccupation until Mora arrived, if she did arrive at all, that is. He began thinking that maybe the whole thing was just a joke on her part, the sort of joke kids used to play on him in school, when they had anything to do with him at all. But she seemed so honest, so earnest. He walked more briskly, and in a few minutes reached the place where they had met. He sat on the same limestone block and cooled down from his walk. He still had an hour or so to wait, so he let himself go into his usual obsessiveness with visual imagery, much like a trance. He didn't hear her steps until she called to him from just a few feet away.

"Carl, you're early. I somehow thought you would be. It's good. We'll have more time together today."

"Oh, hello." He lurched awkwardly around to greet her. "I was just . . ."

"Sorry I startled you. I didn't realize how preoccupied you were. The car is outside. We can go whenever you're ready."

Just as he had done yesterday, the driver got out and opened doors. After they were in the car, and on their way, Mora said, "Carl, there's something you need to know."

Ok, here it comes, he thought to himself. She went on, "I want you to meet a few friends of mine. I think you'll like them They're a lot like you, nice people who haven't made very solid connections with other people, but who are also deeply sensitive. Some are like you, fond of places not visited very often, some are bookish, some like music, and so forth."

"I have to say, I'm not too comfortable in a social setting." His voice was a little edgy.

"I didn't want to tell you yesterday. I thought you might not show up this morning."

"You're probably right. It's not my thing."

"Just come along for now. If you don't like it, then we'll come back early."

"Where is this place?" he asked.

"It's over near Bonvell, about an hour from here. You'll only meet about half a dozen of our group. There are a lot more, and you might want to meet more of them some day. We'll see what you think. Our meeting place today is a little lodge building that's just right for small groups to meet, like we're doing today."

The car, some kind of late model sedan that seemed luxurious, moved over the often ill-kept roads smoothly, with almost no sound from the road. The driver had classical music playing very softly from the several speakers in the car. The landscape, green and lush woods alternating with meadows of grass and flowers, calmed Carl as much as anything Mora could have said. He looked out while she was talking.

Finally he said, "I suppose it's going to be all right. I don't know why, but yesterday I felt I could trust you."

"You can," Mora said. This didn't reassure Carl, who thought of all the people who would say to someone, "Trust me," and then go on to screw them. But before he could become agitated again, the car pulled into a long lane, lined with carefully manicured trees. They came to the end of the road and parked on a gravel path.

The lodge was a carefully architected rustic building, all wood and glass, with views of meadows on one side, woods on the other. Two people were on the porch, and they approached the car as Carl and Mora got out. The driver left immediately, after a signal from Mora. "Hi, gang," she said as they approached the building.

After some greetings and hugs, Mora said, "This is Carl," and went around the group introducing him to Geena, Frank, Orla, and Paolo. "I thought there'd be more, but this is fine," she said.

They went inside, where someone took Carl's gray jacket, asked him to sit, and handed out some drinks. The day had become very warm, too hot to be in the sun for long. But the lodge seemed almost cold. The drink tasted good, and he tried to relax.

"Carl, these are very good friends to me, and I think they will be to you, too. I don't like these awkward times when everybody is greeting each other, but all I can think of now is to go around and let everybody say something about themselves."

Carl felt like running. He hated any kind of involvement like this. But the introductions went on anyway. Mora's friends spoke of what their lives had been before now. Orla told how she was a would-be writer who could never write, spending her days instead alone with books, sometimes reading, sometimes daydreaming. Paolo was much like Carl, taking long solo hikes, sometimes for weeks, in the great western mountains. Frank had hopes of becoming a skilled cellist, but he could never muster the courage to go to an audition. He played sonatas to the deer and rabbits. Geena said she couldn't say anything about what she had done, because it was nothing. She spent nearly every day indoors by a window. Their descriptions of their former lives went on for quite a while, seemingly becoming longer and more articulate as they had more of the drinks that had been poured. Carl had no idea of what the drinks contained, though he was sure they didn't depend on alcohol. Whatever it was, he found it compulsively appealing.

Carl moved close to Mora, "You all seem to know all there is to know about me, but I don't know anything about you, Mora. You didn't say much yesterday. For example, what's your last name?"

Mora hesitated. By the way she interacted with the others, Carl had come to think that she was the leader of the group. But leader of what kind of group? "My background is a little different," she said. "I was in military work. I can't say much more right now, but I'll tell you about it later, when it's the right time. Right now, let's just say my name is Mora S."

Carl would never have guessed Mora to have been an army person, if indeed that's what she was, but he remembered his first impressions of her, and the possibility didn't seem unlikely. With her somewhat masculine features and her slightly coarse voice, it seemed to make sense to him as a subscriber to popular convention in such matters. The drink warmed her up a little more. "Well, if you must know, I served a tour of duty on the front lines, even killing people who we were told were our enemies whenever I was asked. I liked it all, in a way, but I didn't like being nearly the only survivor out of our unit. I couldn't wait to get home. I kicked around doing nothing for a while, then met some people like these guys. It changed my life."

Whenever the glasses became low, Mora would make sure they were replenished. Carl began to feel much closer to these people, and they were clearly trying to make themselves as intimate with him as he would allow. The conversation drifted among personal anecdotes, deep (or so he then thought) philosophical discussions, and contemporary news events. He was impressed by their intimate knowledge of world events, with hints dropped that they knew much more than even the press about inner workings of the political system.

Mora by this time was sitting close to Carl. He talked more and more openly and freely to the group, his usual inhibitions almost vanishing. Mora rested her arm on his leg, and let her hand dangle to the inner part of his thigh. It was intensely stimulating to him, an experience he'd never actually felt, though he had vicariously enjoyed it from erotic material that abounded on the Internet. He didn't react to Mora's apparent invitation, or even acknowledge it, since it just didn't seem to be the direction this group was going.

Geena got up after a while and brought more drinks, this time of a different color. Whatever was in the first drink, it seemed to make Carl feel more at peace with himself than he had been for years. The second drink was more potent. All the obsessions with dark and light that had preoccupied Carl over the years flooded to him in a warm association with the images of his newfound friends, melding it all into an overpoweringly warm feeling of closeness and kinship. He began to feel that he never wanted to leave this lodge. It seemed that no one else did, either. Eventually, Mora got up and remarked that time was going by, and that they should probably have something to eat before making their separate ways.

"Oh my God, oh my God, this is so nice," Carl said. Why he expressed his appreciation in this entirely uncharacteristic way he could not have explained. "Can we meet again?"

"Of course we can," Mora said. "We'll all be leaving shortly, but what you need to do is tell your parents that you're going away to a kind of resort It's called the SOS Estate. That's all you need to say, though you can add that it's a very friendly place filled with people you like, to reassure them. Oh yes, and that you'll be in touch. You're not being kidnapped."

Carl's brain, by now deeply affected by whatever was in the drinks he'd had, registered this proposal as being about the best thing he'd ever heard. In his mind, there was no question whatever about not going to the Estate. Snuggled among Geena, Paolo, Frank, and Orla, with Mora nearby, he felt he had at last reached a place where he was accepted, understood, and desired. The years of rejection melted away, and he could see only a dreamlike future where he was forever part of this warm group.

Mora stood up. "Carl, I think we need to start back. But don't worry, we'll see you again tomorrow."

Everyone got up, saying goodbyes and warmly hugging. Carl didn't feel at all drunk. He knew the drinks were not alcoholic, though he had no idea about what else he may have taken in them. All he wanted now was to make these five people realize how close he was to them, and how he wanted to do whatever was necessary to keep this warmth flowing. He hugged them all and went with Mora to the car.

He got in, and Mora said, "Just a moment, Carl, I left something inside." She went to the door of the lodge. The other four were standing there, preparing to leave. They showed less effect from the drinks than Carl did, as though they were used to them. "Thanks for coming, my friends," Mora said. "I'm sure we have a recruit. The time-release misamine should be good for a couple of days, but I'll leave a little extra with him for tomorrow. I'll see you at the Estate." This was what the SOS camp was now called, a term that had been found to be more reassuring to new recruits than anything with a military-sounding name.

Mora told the driver to go to Carl's home, not to the Zone. On the way, she sat close to him, her arm once more on his leg. Before they left in the morning, he had fantasized that somehow they would become intimate. Now, even though he couldn't bring himself to make the first move, Carl felt immensely satisfied. His head seemed a little muddled, but clear enough for him to know that his life had changed. Somehow, he felt, he would never be able to go back to the Zone, or to a forest, and lose himself in solitude. He would have to become part of a group like the one he had left at the lodge, and go to the Estate.

They pulled up at the house. Mora took out a small plastic box with a pill in it. "Here, this will help you sleep. Please take it tonight. I don't want you to be concerned, and you should be rested for tomorrow. I won't get out with you now, but I'll come early tomorrow morning, about eight. You can say goodbyes to your parents then, and we can leave immediately. Are you happy about what's happened so far?"

"I am. I have to say I liked your friends a lot, but I especially like you. I didn't quite trust you before, but I feel completely different now." Mora was pleased that the misamine was so effective. It made explaining and coaxing unnecessary.

The car left, and Carl went inside. Ed and Lyn were back, puttering around in the kitchen.

"Well, how did it go?" Lyn asked.

Carl didn't know how to answer. The day's events had been entirely different from what he had expected, though his prior expectations now seemed confused. "It was great. She's wonderful. I've never felt so much a part of anything before."

"What's her name, and where did you go?"

"It's Mora. I don't know her last name. We went to meet some friends of hers, fellow SOS members, and hung out with them for most of the day. It was just perfect. I'm going to see them again tomorrow at their headquarters. They call it The Estate."

"Well, good luck," Ed said. Carl thought he was amazingly cool about the whole thing. But Ed hadn't been curious about most of Carl's life so far, so why should he start now?

Lyn was more apprehensive. She tried to ask more about SOS, but Carl could say nothing more about it. Still, his ebullient enthusiasm spilled out, and she seemed somehow reassured. Ed on the other hand, seemed to know more.

"You may decide to join up with the SOS people for good, so it may be a long time before you come back home, Carl. It's been good having you around. I hope it will work out for you." Even in his somewhat dazed condition, Carl thought this was an odd remark, especially since it was the closest to an emotional encounter with his father that he could recall. After a few minutes, he briefly put his hand on Ed's shoulder without saying anything, then turned and went upstairs to his room.

Ed sat quietly for a while, and Lyn nervously toyed with the bottom of her sweater. She seemed on the verge of tears.

"I have to tell you, Lyn," Ed said. "We'll most likely never see him again." Lyn started to cry, but stopped before Ed could reprimand her for being too emotional. The both sat quietly for a while, then they too went to bed.

Chapter 4

The SOS

If U.S. military leaders had learned one single thing after years of futile engagements in the Middle East, it was that the entire strategy for waging wars like those was wrong from the start. The latest debacle arose from a naive and misguided motivation to punish terrorists, bring democracy to the area, and of course insure at the same time a continued flow of oil. The operation turned into a bloodbath that served only to trigger a massive worldwide vendetta by much of the Islamic world toward the West, and cause a loss of U.S. credibility among nearly everyone else. Democracy and the flow of oil seemed equally elusive.

The traditional view for the use of military force held that arms applied in sufficient intensity can conquer any enemy, and the U.S. had maintained this position for years, with mixed success. America's ability to equip land, sea, and air forces had no parallel in history. A massive portion of the budget, even in peacetime, was spent on the development and production of weapons, as well as in training and maintaining armed forces in their use. After World War II, the idea that America had never lost a war gained currency. Later, the country sadly awakened to the experience of several wars that ended either in outright defeat or in dubious standoffs, involving in all cases a lamentable loss of human life.

The seemingly endless battle in Iraq produced a slowly dawning epiphany. Thousands of Americans were slaughtered by an enemy that rarely identified itself and nearly always accomplished its limited mission of death and retaliation with a low casualty rate of its own. The American people were exhausted. Liberals clamored for complete withdrawal and return to a kind of isolationism. Conservatives wanted more fire power, more covert seizure of suspected terrorists, more scrutiny of communications. Theorists and even many elected leaders began to feel that the whole concept of war needed rethinking. Eventually, even the Defense Department publicly declared the struggle a failure. Two presidents were brought to the brink of impeachment for their inept decisions. Gray eminences behind the scene, those who orchestrated the decisions of the president, tried vainly to shore up what little remained of the government's credibility.

In the two so-called Great Wars, the United States felt justified in retaliating against attacks upon its allies or itself. In later wars, the U.S. found itself militarily entering countries for quite different, often questionable, reasons. Korea, Vietnam, and Iraq were all battle locations where many of the people intensely disliked intervention by the U.S. on their home soil. These wars were either lost outright or had ambiguous outcomes. Resistance to the invasion of one's homeland stirs feelings of patriotism and willingness to sacrifice that cannot be compared to fighting on neutral territory. The urge to defend one's homeland is probably hard wired into the human brain, a protective mechanism that caused the U.S. military leaders to rethink the whole theory of war.

There is a sad and repetitious pattern to the way in which traditional wars have been fought. Men and women are sent out in groups called patrols, to encounter their enemy and try to overcome them by superior numbers or by superior weapons. When both sides follow the same ground rules, the side with greater resources usually wins. Historically, when the U.S. was involved, the winner would usually be the Americans though often only after an outrageous loss of human lives.

The attack patrol method is brutally dangerous. Patrols, whether on reconnaissance or in active combat, will have on the average a certain number of deaths and injuries whether they succeed or fail in their missions. Over time, these numbers multiply to become agonizing and even intolerable to those at home. When a clear victory seems elusive, opposition rises on both sides, and eventually one or another of the forces will either withdraw or negotiate a settlement. In either case, the war eventually stops. After a while the countries involved resume friendly economic relations, with a return of tourism and trade, and important memorials are erected to mark the bravery of the fallen troops.

The kind of war fought in Iraq underscored the failure of the traditional patrol and encounter strategy when the setting was on the Iraq homeland. The Iraq "insurgents" developed a quite different battle strategy, having realized that one person willing to voluntarily die for a cause could kill or wound many more than a conventional patrol could take out during a confrontation. The motivations for willingness to die as a "suicide bomber" in this way are a complex mixture of religious beliefs and a desire to defend one's country against outside invaders. Whether the American and allied troops in Iraq saw themselves as liberators, promoters of democracy, guardians of Christianity, or whatever, made no difference. They were seen as invading unbelievers, with their death and demoralization the prime goal of the insurgents.

The idea that one person willing to die for a cause could in turn cause the death or maiming of maybe a score of conventional troops began to be mentioned at nearly every Presidential planning session. The message finally sank into the consciousness of those planning strategy for the administration. It formed the basis for a revelation about, and a revolution in, American soldiery, and led to the creation of the Soldiers of Sacrifice.

The birth of the SOS was no occasion for fanfare. It began as a series of private discussions among the President and a few of his advisors picked for their loyalty and ability to maintain utter secrecy. They had no difficulty in outlining a rough plan for the function of the SOS. They agreed that the assignments of SOS members would never be labeled or spoken of as suicide missions. Instead, the "soldiers" would pose as journalists, writers seeking interviews, business people with proposals, diplomatic staff or a myriad other innocuous occupations. Their mission would be to insinuate themselves closely enough to an undesirable opponent to introduce an armament of lethal and microscopic weapons. They would be sworn to die rather than reveal even the slightest information about the SOS, and to do this by their own hands before any action such as torture could be taken against them. Sometimes, they would be expected to die in carrying out their mission, perhaps in ways not unlike those used by the suicide bombers in Iraq. Dying in the course of an SOS action would be regarded as no different from dying in a hail of bullets on the battlefield, and such a death would be appropriately honored, with generous compensation to relatives and loved ones. The basic idea remained that it would be a much more economical way, in terms of loss of American life as well as actual expense, to wage a war. Removal of opposition leaders rather than engaging masses of troops would seem an obvious course of action.

Initial funding would be no problem. The Defense Department's bloated budget, already accounting for two thirds of the national budget, had countless purses that could be opened for special weapons development and for training. After preliminary drafting of a proposal for the Soldiers of Sacrifice, accompanied by a lot of hand shaking, the President's advisory group realized they had outlined only the bare bones of a plan. Big questions remained about who of these Soldiers would be willing to actually put their lives on the line with every assignment, to be willing to die by their own hands. What kinds of assignments would they take? How would they be trained? How could they know the hundreds of languages of the world well enough to insinuate themselves effectively? How could they develop sufficient political and technical knowledge to infiltrate into the inner workings of world government? A select task force was chosen, with five people of differing skills mandated to produce a working plan. Because of his knowledge of covert electronics, Robert Sikes was one of them, his proven abilities overriding his reputation as a loose cannon.

Brainstorming sessions went on for weeks, with sometimes bitter disagreement, but out of it came a working plan. The basic worldwide mission of the SOS would be the removal of objectionable leaders and any other troublemakers deemed obstacles to U.S. policies. This removal would be by covert means, with military confrontation remaining only as a distant last resort. This decision helped the task force decide the agency where the SOS should be placed. Some had felt it should be under the wing of the DOD, where military operations were normally planned. Because of the importance of secrecy, Robert Sikes wanted it to be part of the Division of Intelligence, run by a selected handful who could be eliminated by any means necessary if they failed to perform. He had a hatred of conventional government, especially the civil service, where it seemed impossible to remove incompetents. He liked to quote a passage he'd written a few years before:

Masses of pathetic failures and misfits, walking and sitting almost aimlessly, cursing their miserably empty lives and the poor decisions that brought them here, but totally incapable of changing or escaping this sad pattern, spending their days in grumbling and complaining rather than occupying themselves with any kind of work that would help the time pass. An insane asylum? A penal farm of some kind? No, the Civil Service.

His forceful campaign won, and the SOS became a secret division of the DI. While it could not be privatized in the conventional sense, the SOS was to be organized and run as a business, with a board of directors able to make changes without outside intervention. The business model demanded that SOS operations show a net "profit," which largely meant a calculation of savings over conventional military operations, especially where human lives were involved. As the SOS gained success, conventional operations would be eliminated. Once these procedures and understandings had been worked out, Sikes threw himself into detailed planning with unparalleled zeal.

Even with 400 million people crowding the cities and towns of America, there were still many isolated places where one could travel for miles, or stay for months, completely alone. The Soldiers of Sacrifice headquarters had been selected to be constructed inside one of them, a ring of mountains in northern California. The mountains had long been privately owned and inaccessible, with very limited road access and a ban on both private and commercial aircraft. Satellite inspection of the site would show nothing more that what seemed to be a country club of isolated buildings connected by vast green spaces and gardens. The location was quickly dubbed "The Estate."

The SOS was to be operated from this single central location, with numerous small "lodges" scattered around the country. These would be used for recruiting, for safe houses, and for small planning sessions. The entire operation would be run by the equivalent of a CEO and a board of directors. Each board member would in turn be director of a subdivision made up of actual Soldiers of Sacrifice. In contrast to conventional military structure, a kind of equality would be practiced among the Soldiers, as well as their leaders. Indiscretion or failure would be punished in ways decided on by peers. No trial or court martial was needed, since any infractions would be known only to other SOS members. Punishment would be swift, and often severe.

The U.S. was still a magnet for immigrants from all over the world, for many reasons. Some sought economic security, some political or religious freedom, some were merely restless or bored, and some genuinely wanted to be part of the mystique that had glued the country together for hundreds of years.   Candidates to the SOS were welcomed from all countries and language groups, and after a rough screening they were closely questioned by other members to weed out unsuitable candidates.   Those who passed this stage were interviewed in more depth by several Soldiers, as close to being peers of the candidate as possible.   Regardless of language, religion or politics, the person being considered would be made to feel warm camaraderie during the interviews. Conducted at a comfortable and rustic lodge, and with the help of mind-altering drugs, the examination identified those candidates who would be welcomed as probationary members of the SOS.

The training they then received would be tiring and difficult, but rarely brutal. Instead, chemical and psychological treatments would be used to insure submission to the objectives of the SOS, and to promote swift and professional completion of assignments. As with other methods of military training, it boiled down to a program of mind alteration. Carl had experienced the first part of this process, and since he had met with approval, he was eager to find out more.

Chapter 5
Robert Sikes

When she and Ed married, Lyn was pregnant with Carl. She was eighteen, and he was five years older. There was no great love that drew them together, but rather the ideological bonding of being young leftists in those idealistic days, a bonding fed by their common hatred of war and of the government responsible for it. This heady dish was further peppered and salted by a newfound freedom of casual sex that some called "free love," and the animal excitement of participating in demonstrations. Ed never seriously intended having a permanent relationship with Lyn at all, but after Carl was born, everything became different. Lyn's attitudes changed drastically, at least where the integrity of the parent-child relationship was concerned. She insisted on having more children, and when Max and Anna were born, she devoted nearly all of her emotional resources to them. Ed liked having the children, but he took care to remain on the outskirts of their rearing. He remained preoccupied with his research efforts and traveling to scientific meetings.

When Ed and Lyn had sex, it was nearly always at her initiation. She suspected he had affairs from time to time on his trips, a belief that was fed by the lessening interest he showed in her over the years. In her youth, she had a startling natural beauty that attracted a flock of admirers, with no shortage of sexual encounters. She met Ed at the pad of a friend they both knew, and it was on a dare while smoking pot that they had gone to a corner of the darkened room to have sex. Ed insisted that she remove all her clothing, though he merely dropped his pants and shorts. The penetration and climax took only a few minutes. He got up, pulled up his pants, stared for a while at her naked body, heaving slightly and glistening with smeared semen, and walked away.

She wondered later why she hadn't insisted on using some protection. She thought that perhaps the pot she had smoked had clouded her reason. In any event, in a month or so she knew she was pregnant. She knew Ed was the only possible father, though he at first thought that one or another of her other "boyfriends" might be responsible. Finally, he agreed that he was indeed the most likely father, and at her insistence they went through the formality of marriage. When it came to her own child, Lyn reverted to an old-fashioned morality, one in which a child is supposed to be born legitimately. Ed, oddly enough considering his own rather philandering tastes, also had a peculiar attachment to the idea that he would be having a child of his own, with his legal surname, and with whatever pains and pleasures all that might entail.

Lyn's second pregnancy produced the twins Max and Anna. After their birth, the frequency of intimate sex between Ed and Lyn dwindled to almost nothing. She still had her youthful beauty, and her youthful sexual desires, so the problem of temptation became tangible to her. Ed never let on that he might have any such desires, though she was convinced that he found satisfaction in some way while he was away from home. His feeble denials only deepened their sexual rift.

When Robert Sikes entered their lives, Lyn's feelings of sexual dissatisfaction with Ed seemed to peak, as did her latent sexual passions. Robert was younger than Ed, and quite handsome. Women who knew him were unaware of his deepening mental problems, and thought of him merely as quaintly charming. Tall and muscular, with close-cropped hair and a tanned Mediterranean look, he resembled a kind of ideal military man. He had never been in an armed force, since the Vietnam draft ended before he was old enough, but he claimed he wouldn't have objected had he been called to serve.

When Robert Sikes and Ed Grendil met, they realized that each had something to offer the other, although their wildly different backgrounds and personalities made it unlikely that they would see eye to eye on anything other than their technical work. Their meetings were as infrequent as Ed could make them, usually occurring at Ed's house or on even more neutral ground. They exchanged what information was necessary for the work to proceed, and that was that. When Lyn was around, Sikes watched her closely, partly because he was aroused by her beauty, and partly to try to fathom her relationship with Ed. It wasn't hard for him to conclude that she and Ed were almost like married strangers.

After their F-chip project was completed and launched, and the DOD funds were rolling in, Ed and Robert felt little need to see or talk to each other at all. Their distance turned into outright avoidance, and the meetings at Ed's home when he could ogle Lyn almost faded away. Nevertheless, he still thought often of her. Finally, when he knew that Ed was away on a lengthy trip and that the children would be in school, he dropped by the house. She was surprised, but not at all displeased, at seeing him. She made coffee, and they chatted at the breakfast table. She had dressed very casually to do housework, in a loose tee shirt with no bra, and shorts. Robert could not keep his eyes from the nipple outlines on her shirt.

In spite of his obsession with physical theory, computers, and math, Robert still found himself driven by a hormonal obsession with sex. In high school, and even part of the time in college, he was pretty much the loner. In spite of his good looks, he was often regarded as the school nerd, and he generally escaped the notice of the "sex bitches" that were clearly giving a lot of the other students "good lays." He had no interest in courting a "nice" girl but looked for uncomplicated and intense sexual encounters. He had tried going to one or two of the local prostitutes but had found them to be so coarse, and maybe even unclean and infected, that he gave up. The girls he did have sex with were much like him, hot and passionate but unfulfilled. By the time high school ended, he was an experienced casual lover. He saw Lyn merely as someone who would enjoy fucking. He had no interest in carrying on a "meaningful" conversation or anything else with her.

He watched her closely as she poured the coffee. After he had taken a couple of sips, he put down his cup, slid his chair closer to hers, and put his hand on one of her breasts. "I want you, Lyn," he said.

She was startled but not repelled. She drew back slightly without removing his hand. "I don't know, Rob. You know my situation."

"I know enough to realize that you would like to be with a man and that man isn't likely to be your husband."

"Actually, Rob, I've thought about you, too."

Now he was the startled one. He hadn't expected it to be so easy. He pulled her toward him and kissed her. She returned his kiss ardently, letting her arm slide between his legs.

"Let's go to the bedroom," she said.

She removed her clothes so quickly that she had time to help Robert remove his. They lay together on the large bed, panting and shaking a bit in anticipation, before he rolled over onto her outspread legs. He paced himself, and they alternatively coupled and rested for nearly half an hour. Finally, both were spent, and they lay on their backs.

"That was so good," she said. "It's not been this way for me for a long time."

"I thought so. I could see how you two get along. I suppose you stay with him because of the children."

"Yes, that's partly it. The truth is, I like some things about Ed. We're on the same wavelength with politics and stuff like that."

"Yes, I suppose you would be," he said. "You were both hippies together."

"Yes, we were in a way. But we would both have been like that without the other. I just can't stand the way this country has become obsessed with wanting to use arms to change the world."

"Well, I don't want to get into that discussion. I like you, and want to keep it that way. I don't like Ed, mainly because we've locked horns on those kinds of political things before.

We're totally   opposite to each other. I like what the government's doing. Maybe we should just leave it at that."

She became quiet. If she were a smoker, this would have been the moment to light up, stare blankly at the ceiling and at the curling smoke. Instead, she just said, "I will never mention it again."

"Again?" he asked. "Would you like for me to drop in again?"

"Yes."

He kissed her lightly, sat on the bed and put his clothes back on. "I don't know when," he said. "Maybe you could let me know about Ed's trips. I'll give you a private phone number where you can always reach me."

"I'll do that," she said.

For several days afterward, Lyn found herself thinking about her encounter with Robert. It had been pleasant, almost unbearably so, for her. But the ramifications kept nagging at her. He and Ed were, after all, partners, and he was, after all, a hard-line right winger, her avowed enemy.

In their earlier years together, Lyn and Ed had tried to be open and honest with each other and she remembered how good it felt to be free of guilt. So, one evening, at dinner, she decided to tell Ed something about her encounter with Robert. Without elaborating on any details, she let it be known that he was more than interested in her sexually and that he wanted to see her again. She wasn't in the least contrite, nor did Ed act surprised.

He sat back quietly for quite a while, and finally said, "You probably don't realize it, but Sikes has some serious problems."

"I know about his politics, and his dislike of you. Is there anything else?"

"Well, I haven't seen any diagnosis, but I think he's on the border of insanity. I even wonder if he might become violent."

Lyn didn't respond. Her view of Sikes was quite different, but she had no other information.

Ed went on, "I'm not happy about suggesting this, but his interest in you gives us a good opportunity for something that might come in very handy one day for the Reform Party. I think he hates me enough to try to get at me in some way, maybe even try to destroy me. It may be useful if we could get something on him that could be revealed if we needed it. Would you help?"

"I didn't think you would react this way, exactly," she said. "Aren't you the least bit jealous?"

"Lyn, let's face it. You and I don't have much of a life together. We get along, support the kids, and all that. Of course I feel something when someone like Robert makes a pass at you. But you're a good-looking woman, and I'd bet this isn't the first time."

"No, Ed, it isn't," she lied. It was true that she had flirted and kissed a bit after their marriage, but nothing seriously sexual had come of it. The encounter with Robert Sikes was different. She had a growing suspicion that Ed used his trips for one night stands, and she was painfully aware that her days of being sexually attractive were not going to last forever. With the realization that their once intense sexual attraction to each other was vanishing, she found herself more and more indifferent to remaining faithful.

"Well, what do you think about helping set Robert up?"

"It's not how I thought I'd end up as a desirable woman, but if it could help, I suppose so."

Ed asked her to let him know she planned to get together with Sikes again. During the days following, she wavered time and again about making the call. The whole thing was so shoddy. She wanted to tell Ed that it was off, that she couldn't do it. But then again, what was so bad about it? Robert Sikes was not important to her. She had enjoyed the animal sex of their first encounter, but if she really wanted to do that sort of thing there were many men available, men closer to her in nearly every way.

At last, she moved to the phone to call Robert. "Can you come over early this afternoon?" she asked.

"I'll try. What time? Where's Ed?"

"He's on a trip. I don't expect him back. I'll be here. Would about one be ok with you?"

Robert hadn't thought too much about Lyn since their first time, though when he did he felt a surge of arousal. He knew she would telephone but couldn't guess when, so he was hardly surprised when she called. The time she suggested seemed awkward. The children would be getting home from school around four. He would have to be gone long before that, but being with her again was worth the risk. He was more drawn to her than he cared to admit to himself.

She met him at the door, fully dressed. They kissed, and went into the living room. "I want you to do something a little different, Robert."

"Ok, what is it?"

"I'd like for you to rape me. You know, take a knife and threaten me with it until I take off my clothes."

As he had been before, he was surprised by her forwardness. He had fantasized about raping someone before, so the idea seemed stimulating to him. "That's a new one for me. I like it."

"Go into the kitchen and get a knife. I'll just stay here like I am. When you come out, just go through whatever you think you would have to do to get me to submit." As he left, she flipped a switch near the door that turned on a security video camera in the room, to make a record of all that went on.

Sikes returned with a kitchen knife. When Lyn saw it in his hand, Ed's remark about his near insanity made her think she had gone too far. He had become visibly aroused, and the whole idea of taking her by force seemed to excite him even more. He ran quickly toward her. "Take off your clothes," he demanded.

She feigned fear quite convincingly. She took off her shoes, and unbuttoned her shirt, fumbling a bit, acting as though nervousness was preventing her fingers to coordinate.

"Faster, you bitch" he said.

She stripped to her bra and panties, and cowered with genuine fear. "Take it all off, right now," he said, removing his own clothing.

When they were both naked, he told her to lie on the couch. He still held the knife in one hand. Their sex together was much wilder than it had been the first time. She was relieved when he dropped the knife, and she screamed with pleasure as he plunged between her legs. In just a few minutes it was over. They were still joined when the front door clicked loudly. There, glaring at them, was Ed.

"You bastard," he said. "I never did trust you."

"She asked for it," Sikes said. "If anything it was her idea."

Ed lunged at him, tried to land a blow, and fell onto the floor, apparently hitting his head on the edge of a table. He didn't move.

Sikes didn't want to know Ed's condition. He quickly dressed, and told Lyn that she had to explain everything to Ed. The simulated rape, her desire, the whole thing. He ran to the door to leave.

"Don't worry, Robert, I'll take care of it," she said almost casually.

When Robert left, Ed got up and sat on the couch. "That was a nasty blow. It could have knocked me out if I'd been an inch to the left. Are you ok?"

"I'm ok," she said. "But I'm surprised you waited so long to come in. I was afraid."

"Well, you seemed to be enjoying it so much. It reminded me of the old days back in the communes."

"Oh, I thought you were the one who was enjoying it vicariously."

"Well, maybe a little bit. You were so excited. But that's beside the point. The main thing is we have the whole thing on film, and it will look very convincing indeed. I think we will have Robert where we want him when or if the time comes."

"I'm glad you got your movie. Just don't sit around with your cronies looking at it. And, for your information, Ed Grendil, I did enjoy it." She was still completely naked, and took a long time to make her way to the shower.

Ed found himself quite aroused by the whole event. He stripped and followed Lyn into the shower room, eliciting a girlish laugh from her when she saw how excited he was. She was wet and soapy as he pulled her toward him and straddled her on the wash basin, thrusting with long and deliberate strokes. A little later they went back into the shower together and embraced for a long time in the warm water, feeling a closeness that had slipped away from them years before.

Chapter 6
At Headquarters

His sudden and embarrassing naked exposure to an irate Ed was humiliating to Sikes, though to his thinking it must have been much more painful for Ed. He was wholly unaware that the whole scene with Lyn had been filmed. He avoided both Ed and Lyn for a year or so after that incident, while he went on to develop elaborate plans for the SOS. His dislike of Ed and his communistic politics gradually hardened into a hatred, though without any contact it didn't go beyond than that. In his mind, which became more and more deranged, he began to develop the idea of getting back at Ed through his son Carl, and maybe Lyn as well.

Carl Grendil knew Robert Sikes, of course, but he had hardly spoken to him during the years he came to the house to confer with Ed on business. Least of all would he know anything of Sikes's involvement in the formation and planning of the SOS. Sikes, on the other hand was fully aware when Carl was being "drafted" by Mora and her friends. His association with Ed Grendil had long been severed, which suited him, since there was nothing else Ed could contribute that could be of any use to him. He had moved along with the technology much farther than Ed could ever dream of doing, using it to design many of the secretive procedures of the SOS. He left the training, organizational, and funding matters to others, but he wanted to be in on every aspect of secret operations. This was not difficult for him to arrange. His track record in producing helpful devices and procedures had been nearly flawless, and, except for his quirky personality, his personal life was unremarkable. He acted as though he was born to serve the SOS. He might have risen to the top of the DI were it not for a few colleagues who recognized in him some disturbing mental traits, not the least being a persistent paranoia that seemed to spoil any efforts of others to become close to him.

When Carl became part of the organization, it had been in full operation for six years, with an impressive record of successes. The original planners were careful not to leave a paper trail of aims, procedures, internal structure, names of leaders and Soldiers, or any details of their successful operations other than a few encrypted computer files. These organizational matters were conveyed orally to new members, and reviewed periodically by experienced peers to make sure everyone worked from the same ground rules.

Carl had left home with some misgivings, but on the whole he looked eagerly toward this new experience, one which had already given him at the lodge the most intense feeling of warmth and friendship he had felt in his whole life. The large dose of misamine he got there had mostly worn off, but the pills Mora asked him to take later maintained an effective level, and he felt he wanted more involvement. She was careful to give him no details about what awaited him, though in her seemingly guileless way she often implied that it would be a happy and satisfying time for him. As they drove to the entrance of the Estate, whatever slight worries he had vanished. It did indeed look like a resort, with an imposing replica of a corbeled Mayan arch extending across the gateway. The gate opened automatically from a device in the car. The road that led toward the Estate headquarters building was artfully curved, passing small sculpted ponds, and clumps of trees and shrubs that were entirely unfamiliar to him.

Mora accompanied him to a small office just inside the entrance. It was dwarfed by the entry space. There was no receptionist, but a jovial looking woman rose immediately from her desk to greet him. "Hello, Carl," she said. "We've known you were coming. Have a seat. I'm Thalia M'Gos, director of the Estate." Carl was a little surprised to be introduced to the leader right away, but it seemed a nice touch.

Mora continued standing and finally said, "Now that Carl is in good hands, I think I'll go back to my house to catch up on messages. I may not see you for a while, Carl, but I'm sure we'll be able to meet again."

With that, she nodded to Thalia, and left. The director turned to Carl with a smile, "I pronounce my name 'magoss,' to make things easy. My original African name is even harder, so I shortened it to this to keep a little touch with my roots.

We usually don't use real last names here. I think you'll realize why pretty soon." Her skin was a creamy brown, her face set off by dark black hair pulled smoothly back, and deeply penetrating brown eyes. Now about forty years old, she had been director of the Estate for four years, having started just the way Carl was starting, as a new recruit. Carl found later that the previous director died while on an important mission.

Carl couldn't think of anything to say that wasn't trivial. "I'm happy Mora brought me here. I suppose I'll find out how I fit in later."

"We don't like to rush things too much, though it may seem like it. We'd like for you to have a physical exam and get a couple of shots, and then you'll be free to roam around until dinner. You might want to watch the orientation video in your room. There's plenty of time to fill you in with all the details."

"I'm just curious. How many people are there in the SOS?"

Thalia hesitated for a bit. "It varies," she said. "I can't give you an exact figure right now, but usually it runs to about 500. Many of the Soldiers are away on various assignments. I doubt that there are more than half around the Estate right now. You'll probably meet some of them after you have your physical. They can fill you in a bit more. But now let me escort you to the exam room."

They left her small office, and re-entered the high-ceilinged entry space, crossing diagonally to a glass door leading to a room intensely lit with LED lamps. "I'll say so long here for a while, Carl. We'll no doubt see each other at dinner."

Carl felt a little apprehensive about the vagueness of the encounter with Thalia, and even worried about what his part in the organization might be, but just when Thalia left the room, two medically-robed people entered. The man said, "Hey, Carl. I'm Robby. This is Maria." Their smiles and easy manners put him at ease.

Robby said, "Why don't you take off all your things and put them in this box. You won't need them anymore, since we have a whole set of new clothes for you. I think you'll like how you look."

They didn't leave the room, and Carl was a little embarrassed at being naked in front of them like that, but they were both involved in preparing solutions and reading various electronic instruments operated from a large panel. "Go ahead and lie on the table," Maria said.

They passed various sensors over his entire body, crisscrossing in all directions. Carl could see from computer screens that they were obtaining a highly detailed map of his entire body structure, and probably every aspect of its condition. "We'll need to do a little more later, but this is enough for now," Robby said. "Now, we need to give you a couple of shots. Nothing to worry about."

The syringes were quite small and the administration of the shots proficient. After the first one, Carl looked up at Robby and Maria and tried to speak, "I . . . feel . . ." His voice dropped. After the second shot, he was completely unconscious.

He was wheeled into a surgery chamber, where a masked surgeon awaited. He deftly made an incision into the center of Carl's palm, and implanted a small chip. This version of the F-chip was intended as an emergency communication device by which the SOS leaders could communicate with the Soldiers. The Fourier transform signals of course made it impossible for an outsider to realize that transmission was occurring. In a rather more complex operation, the surgeon fashioned another F-chip into a cochlear implant. The pair of chips became a complete communication system. By placing an implanted palm over the ear, both chips became activated to pick up and transmit audio signals, as well as to receive them silently and directly into the receptors of the ear. Carl would be told about this device later.

After embedding the chips, the surgeon contacted another SOS person about whether to proceed with the next stage. He learned that the kind of assignments Carl would receive would not likely be complex or dangerous enough to require the use of the SOS's more sophisticated neural nanoelectronic devices, called neurobots. These were tools under development by a group led by Sikes, and included devices to block pain under torture, or in some cases to alter basic personality traits. The procedures to use them were not without risk. The insertion of nanoelectronic devices into the brain involved injecting them into the carotid artery, where they could be propelled and implanted into any desired part of the brain by monitoring their position on detailed scans. When installed and activated, the bots integrated themselves into the brain function seamlessly. Unfortunately, though rarely, the bots erred sufficiently in location and intended function to cause permanent personality alteration. There was no effective way to communicate with the bot, or to remove it. Drastic electrical shock might sometimes deactivate it, but by then, brain damage would already have occurred.

None of this was even slightly apparent to Carl when he woke up. The surgeon explained to him, "We just installed a very advanced form of two-way communication. I'm sure you will find it very useful when you are on an assignment."

"Nobody said anything to me about assignments. What kind of assignments?"

"There will be plenty of time for you to learn about all that. The only thing we're doing here is just getting you ready in a very basic kind of way. For now, just rest up. Here, have a drink of this."

Carl sipped from a glass. It was the same color and taste of the liquid Mora had given him at the lodge. In a few minutes, his worry about assignments or why he was there vanished. He felt ready to take on anything, and had no qualms whatever about whether to trust the SOS members he had met so far.

Maria said, "Well, it looks like you're back to normal. Here's a robe and some sandals. You can go next door and get fitted for some new clothes. Then you can go to see your rooms. We'll probably see you around. Oh, yes. Here are some pills for you to take along. They're just to make you feel a little better. Take one whenever you have an urge to."

He was left alone. The room next door hardly resembled a haberdashery, just a couple of tables with picture books of clothing strewn over them. A man entered and introduced himself as Jim. "So, Carl, some new clothes."

All of Carl's measurements were already on line in the computer. The tailor made a couple of confirmatory measurements with a tape, and then opened one of the books. "This is about how we think you'd like to look." The picture showed a young man wearing the typical clothing of a suburban Californian of the time. Khaki pants, a dark shirt, black shoes, and a casual jacket with no tie. "We'll give you several outfits like this. They'll all be slightly different, but you can interchange everything." Jim opened a side door where the new clothing was hanging.

Carl put on his custom clothes, and admired his image in a mirror. He was surprised at how much better properly fitted clothing looked. Maria was outside when he left the tailor, or whatever Jim might have called himself, since Carl had already learned that SOS people were likely to be highly versatile.

"You look pretty sharp," she said. "I'll take you to your rooms. We assign our people to private rooms, but there's no restriction about having other Soldiers visit or even stay over. You'll find that there will be others that you like a lot here, probably that have your same interests."

Carl didn't want to elaborate on this, since by his own evaluation he didn't seem to have many interests at all. An obsession with taking photos of light and dark patterns, and a halfway serious interest in science history. That was about it. His shyness and feelings of inadequacy would have returned except for the drink he'd had, and now the pills. He had no idea at the time, but misamine was one of several drugs given to the SOS on a regular basis, drugs that caused both profound and subtle personality changes. Most were combined with a fast addicting alkaloid, so that future dosing was self-activated, at least for Soldiers living at the Estate or on assignments that were not too long. For those who would be away for long times, or in situations where taking a pill would not be possible, the neurosurgeons were experimenting with constant improvements in permanent brain alterations using implanted nanobots.

The rooms were simple, though finished with taste to give a feeling of restrained luxury. Tinted glass brought a suffused light into areas of dark siding and hardwood floors covered with attractive rugs. The two rooms were spacious. One was the bedroom and bath and the other a study and library, with a striking view of the estate grounds that would encourage contemplative study. A couple of landscape paintings were on the wall, and a few small sculptures on shelves. Maria seemed proud of the quarters. "I love these rooms," she said. "Quiet, restful." Just then someone came to the open door with a delivery of the rest of Carl's clothing, minor variations of what he had already been issued.

Maria opened the door to leave. "See you for dinner in a couple of hours. Just touch the screen to get a video menu."

Carl sat still for some time, then toyed with the video screen. He had never been much of a fan of this medium, but it was almost the only thing in his room that could be used for passing the time. There were no books or magazines. The image on the screen was an unfamiliar face, and he didn't realize for a while that it was animation, superlatively done. "Welcome Carl," the voice said. A slight pause after "welcome" tipped him that he was hearing a computer-generated voice. "I hope everything is comfortable for you. Before you go to dinner, I'd like to give a brief rundown of what you will be doing tomorrow. Oh, my name is Jonas. I'm Thalia's assistant, in charge of new arrivals. There have been six of you checking in today. That's about our average weekly recruitment. You will meet some of them at dinner. Tomorrow you will begin your lessons. The classes will go on all day for a few months, maybe more depending on what kind of assignment you will be given. The people here at the Estate are a wonderful bunch. You will like them." Carl wondered to himself why he was being told this by everyone, and why dinner seemed to be the big focal point of the day.

Jonas went on. "The purpose of Soldiers of Sacrifice is to carry out the missions of America in the most economical possible way, not only economical in finances, but in human costs. In the last large war the U.S. was involved in, the one in Iraq, the country learned several lessons. One of the main ones was how effective the suicide bombers of the enemy could be. As you know, in the last several wars fought by this country, the loss of life has been unacceptably large. In their wisdom, the leaders of the country have decided that an armed force should be used only in case of attack on the country, with most other operations carried out by methods suggested by the Iraqi insurgents. These methods would be implemented by the Soldiers of Sacrifice. This is not to say that the crude methods of the suicide bombers would be adopted, but instead far more sophisticated means, almost beyond imagination. You are becoming a member of the most effective weapon the United States has ever had.

"You may wonder just who are the Soldiers of Sacrifice, or SOS as we usually say, or sometimes just Soldiers. As you know, America is a multicultural society, with hundreds of different ethnic and cultural divisions, with as many national languages being spoken, and as many local cultural mores being maintained. We recruit from these people, just as we did you. Your group, drawn from our basic white community, is as important to us in missions within the country as the multis are to our international missions. While those operations may account for most of our activity, we feel that our work within the country is just as important."

Carl was waiting for the main message. When it came, he was startled, though the misamine made sure he would not become uneasy.

"You may also be wondering just what is the mission of SOS. In a nutshell, it is to remove from active participation anyone in the world who is regarded as a direct threat to the objectives of the United States. These objectives involve economic dominance of the American democracy over a world of local dictatorships and false democracies. It is the U.S. aim to keep these governments decentralized and destabilized. Any leader attempting to organize opposition to the U.S. objectives becomes a target for removal by the SOS.

"Our Soldiers, the members of SOS, are very special people. They have received the most intensive training possible today. You, as one of them, will be fully trained to carry out your mission. This training will include how you receive your orders, how to equip yourself for the job, how to find your way to the target site, how to make yourself part of the target community, how to facilitate the final assignment, how to escape, and, equally important, how to separate yourself from a painful prospect of torture should you be captured, or should the mission fail. Failure is not one of the options of the SOS, so if you are brought back to the Estate alive after failure, you will have to undergo lengthy retraining, plus some form of punishment administered by your friends and colleagues, the severity depending on how they judge you. You will see one such punishment after tonight's dinner.

"I know, Carl, that all this sounds a little vague and perhaps intimidating. But in nearly all cases our Soldiers return from their assignments with glorious success, and usually live to carry out several other missions. It is all very exciting when you are involved in it, and the honor of serving in this way, to be part of such a close group, is a great one. We have estimated that one SOS action, with the loss of one

Soldier, is the equivalent of a hundred or more men involved in conventional combat in either accomplishing a mission or failing at it. Our success rate is high, and our loss of life is very small compared to the loss in direct military confrontation.

"So, Carl. You can watch something else on the video if you like. Or just loll around a bit until dinner. After we have eaten, you will see a punishment. It's not supposed to be a threat, but just a reminder of how we see our duty. I appreciate your coming to SOS. It has been a pleasure speaking to you."

Carl felt drawn almost obsessively to the speaking figure of Jonas. The words were rousing, and he felt a frisson of anticipation for what he may be doing for the SOS. He had not been a great reader of history, or even of the current daily papers, but he did know that a huge sea change had occurred in the way the U.S. conducted its wars. There was almost no mention of military interventions anymore, nor daily body counts of the deaths of Americans or even of their enemies. He knew that the U.S. still had enemies, but obviously the ways of dealing with them had changed drastically. Had he been more cognizant of the daily press, he would have realized that in the past few years, military actions involving troops were only a tenth of those in former years. Instead, when some region of the world became "hot," as the DI people liked to say, it was nothing short of amazing how, within a short time of weeks or months, those responsible for the trouble would just disappear.   Occasionally there would be announcements of their deaths, but more often, they were simply never heard from again. Their replacements would be showered with favors from the U.S., and usually they would profess an agreeable pro-U.S. attitude almost immediately. If not, they themselves would mostly likely disappear. Of course, no one connected with these SOS operations ever gave even a hint of what had happened, except rarely during certain ceremonies. Carl, like the rest of the public, would be left almost completely in the dark. Their infiltration into nearly any important region of the world, and the removal of certain "difficult" people, was the chief, and ultra-secret, mission of the Soldiers of Sacrifice. They used any method available to carry it out.

Chapter 7
Dinner

Just as he had been told, everyone Carl had met so far at the Estate turned up for dinner in the huge dining room. Several hundred people were there, but the space was large enough to accommodate at least three times that many. The multiethnic variety of the guests was impressive, resembling a social session of the General Assembly, at least when the UN was still functioning. Carl was promptly seated among a group of people close to his own age. He assumed they were the recruits who had come to the Estate that week. Introductions went around, but Carl only half heard them. Never good at associating names and faces, his new acquaintances quickly became a blur. After some unusual cocktails that were reminiscent of an exotic fruit punch, though in this case not alcoholic, dinner was brought out. He sensed it was an excellent meal, one that his fellow diners would consider to be delicious. He was largely indifferent to the quality of food and drink, thanks to the everyday meals prepared by Lyn and Ed that would hardly enhance anyone's appreciation for food.

He asked the others at the table if they had heard the message of Jonas on the video. They all had. No one volunteered any comments about it, and let the topic drop. Most of the table conversation was about what they had studied in school in years past, what their family and friends were like, and a smattering of other personal but neutral topics.

At the close of dinner, glasses were clinked and Thalia got up to speak.

"Dear Soldiers, it is always an unhappy duty of mine to have to preside over the punishment of one of us who has transgressed in his or her duties. But it is one of the rules of our group. Our duty is to our country, to carry out projects that are designed to make it stronger, more self reliant, and less threatened by those who would aim at our destruction. I am sorry to have to report that one of our Soldiers, Keena, failed in her project in such a way as to jeopardize the secrecy and integrity of our program. On assignment in Asia, she decided at the last moment that she could not carry out her mission and began trying to explain our operation to strangers. Luckily for us, she was regarded as having mental problems, and was taken to a psychiatric unit for investigation. She was examined closely, and thankfully those present were not sufficiently alert to recognize any of our tools on her person. We were able to purchase her removal and bring her back here. We all liked Keena, and it is with regret that I have to turn her over now to a group of her peers for punishment. Later she will spend at least six months in retraining."

Everyone in the room, if they had not already finished their meal, stopped eating, and sat transfixed. Keena was brought out to the center of the room, wearing a thin robe. She was surrounded by her peers, who had been her closest friends. One of them, close to tears, explained how they had reached their decision about Keena's punishment. They took into consideration her shyness and modesty, and decided that something intensely humiliating would be appropriate, combined with enough physical pain to make her acutely aware that she had come perilously close to the ultimate penalty of death. An important part of these punishments was the forceful lesson left with all present. They, and especially Keena, would never forget the experience.

Her ordeal began when her outstretched arms were tied to a bar running above a platform in the center of the room, clearly placed there just for the purpose of punishment. Keena's face was drawn and white with fear, in anticipation of what was to come. Her peers stripped her of her robe, cutting away the arms and leaving her complete naked. She closed her eyes as if to try to hide, but this in no way diminished the pain she felt in her debased position. The room was not hot, but lines of sweat began to appear on her body. A deeply resonant drum beat had started softly at the beginning of the punishment, and now it increased in loudness in a slow and measured way.

At a signal, a man came to the platform, masked but shirtless to reveal a powerful muscularity. He brought a short knotted whip, which he casually showed to the still silent audience. He looked over Keena's body, beautifully formed with no visible blemishes. Her pale flesh now glistened all over with sweat. Then he took a position to one side, and with no warning, administered the first blow. The shock of this first pain was more than whatever Keena may have expected and she screamed. Her punisher began regular blows, in time with the drum, which had by now become almost unbearably loud. Keena began wildly dancing around the platform, futilely trying to escape the blows, screaming and crying, her breasts moving rhythmically as she leapt and gyrated. Blood spattered the surface of the platform. The sadistic eroticism of the scene was obvious to all, but even those who had thought that the SOS would never condone such a punishment viewed it in complete silence.

Her tormentor kept a close watch on her, and just before she passed out with pain, he stopped. A slight murmur from the spectators seemed to signify that she had suffered enough. The man bowed slightly, then left the room. Keena remained hanging. The diners had long since lost whatever appetite they may have had, and simply sat to wait out the end of the ordeal. Her friends began to take her down after a time, draping her bleeding body with a towel, and helping her from the room. She would be washed and taken to the infirmary for recovery and observation. It would take several days for her to be able to begin her second phase of punishment, a long retraining session considered to be more difficult than that given to new recruits.

During all this, the room had been nearly silent. The sexual overtones of the punishment were obvious, but instead of arousing anyone, those who watched seemed stunned by Keena's agony and humiliation. Thalia returned to the podium. Her eyes were moist. She liked Keena, and had never cared for these punishment sessions. "Keena is very fortunate," she told the group. "Thanks to the mercy of her peers, her punishment was not severe, by no means life threatening. When she recovers, and undergoes some further training, she will be given another opportunity to serve. But I remind you that she will not have a third chance. Now, Soldiers, enjoy your dessert, and have a pleasant evening."

Carl, still under the influence of misamine placed into the food, or in the pills he had started taking, was awed by the whole proceeding, but not appalled or even surprised. Before the SOS, he would have been utterly shocked by the punishment. His mental capabilities of independent reasoning had now become sublimated into a warm and almost loving acceptance of all the Soldiers he had met and whatever they believed in and stood for. He was overwhelmed with a desire to become intimately close to the group, and seemed to take away from the punishment a reinforcement of the closeness of the Soldiers that was the very backbone of the entire SOS. Violating the trust of the group would create a quite logical reason for punishment, even death. It seemed the natural way.

After dinner, most people left to return to their rooms. The entertainment for those who remained was a short piano recital by one of the Soldiers, who announced that she would play a piano sonata by Elliott Carter. The music, once avant garde, now seemed quaint and almost old fashioned. Carl did not recognize the particular work, though he knew it was Carter. He had no musical ability himself, but his parents had often played recordings of modern works at home, and he developed a taste for them. During the performance, someone came to sit near him. He turned and saw it was Mora, whom he hadn't seen since his arrival. She smiled, and took his hand. Later, she told him, "I saw you over here. I hadn't realized that you liked modern music."

"I recognized Carter, but not that piece. Funny how something that once seemed so difficult turns out later to be such easy listening."

"I have a lot of this kind of music on my computer. Maybe you can come over one evening and hear it."

"I'd like that. I'm not sure how things work here, so if you say it's ok, then I'll come."

"Of course it's ok. This is a community of like-minded people with a mission. It's not a prison camp or anything like that."

He laughed. "But I'd bet that now that I've signed on, I couldn't just walk out the gate."

"You can. Many of us come and go all the time, on some project or other. Naturally, if you left as an antagonist, with some intention of harming the SOS, then, well, that would be different."

"Don't worry. All I want to do is make myself useful. How long will it be before I get an assignment?"

Mora frowned a little. "You're a long way from that now. There's a lot of training in what we're all about, how we accomplish missions, how we avoid detection, all that. It's pretty complicated. By the end of the training, I guarantee you'll know things you never imagined."

"Why don't we walk for a while? I can find out where your rooms are." He wanted to extend his visit as much as he could.

They went outside. The air was cool and damp. Mora held on to Carl's hand. No doubt because of the drugs he was taking, this seemed to be contact enough, and he made no effort to become physically closer. Before he had come to the Estate, at the time when he first met Mora, he was almost overcome with desire for her, fantasizing about how it would be to sleep with her. Now his sexual enthusiasm for her had diminished for reasons he could not understand, although he was even more sure that she was available, and willing.

"Mora, there's one thing I've wondered about. Why me? There must be hundreds of people around who would be as good or better SOS candidates."

"I told you, Carl, that I'd had my eye on you since we were in school together. You've got a great mind, at least when you make use of it. If we have a chance we can explore all that together. I know you can become a good Soldier. Besides, I liked the way you look."

Her candor surprised Carl, and made him feel uncertain about how he should proceed. He took an easy way out.

"Mora, I guess I'm a little tired after all that's happened today. I think I'll turn in."

They were not far from his rooms. "Ok, Carl," she said. "You will be really busy from now on, so we probably won't see each other too much. But if you need something, call me."

She abruptly turned and went in another direction. He saw that she joined three others nearby who walked away slowly with her. Carl went inside his apartment and tried not to think more about her.

The three strollers had been waiting for her. After greeting them, Mora spoke to Frank, who had been one of the four Soldiers that helped Mora recruit Carl in the lodge. "Have you heard from Robert Sikes?"

"Not yet," Frank replied, "But the last time we met, he wanted to make sure that we give Carl a lot of special attention. I think he wants to have him trained for a project sooner than the rest of us have been."

Chapter 8
The Reform Party

To the surprise and shock of the two principal political parties, Ed Grendil's Reform Party was able to obtain enough petition signatures to enter primaries in nearly every state, with Ed as presidential candidate. For months, mostly at his own expense, he had spoken to people all over the country, no matter how small the audience. After even a few such talks, he was astounded at the number of volunteers wanting to spread the word themselves, or to help out in other ways. He had put together a pamphlet describing the platform, with frank appraisal of what seemed realistic and what might be just something to hope for. Those who rallied to help had a vast range of skills, and they came from every niche and income level of society, from field workers to university presidents. Surprising to all was the surge of candidates for Congress who wanted to align themselves with the Reform Party.

The platform for the party, now usually called just the RP, was fairly simple, at least to Ed. He wanted nearly all the government functions that had been privatized in recent years to be restored under a new kind of government control, one that differed significantly from the old bureaucratic model. He felt strongly that the people who benefit from government services should determine how they are run, in contrast what she saw as control by highly paid executives and politicians who rarely have need for those services themselves. The amount of money available for social programs would be that remaining from tax income after essential functions of government had been accommodated. Direct involvement of voters in spending programs was essential. With grants dispensed according to peer-determined needs of the recipients, there would be a vast reduction in bureaucratic decisions by officious clerks. The immediate reaction from the entrenched parties was that the RP was simply another name for socialism, offering a stale plan that had a history of failure. Ed and his followers of course disagreed, believing that whatever had been called socialism before had never had direct popular input.

One day, while he described this plan, Lyn asked, "I don't understand all this, Ed. What would prevent your public benefactors from just simply voting to give themselves all the money in, let's say, the social security fund?"

"We're not talking about just throwing money into the air after some citizen has a problem. The disbursal mechanism would change, but we're not changing the constitution. It's just that it would be more direct, rather than filtering through a lot of appointed bureaucrats. Your house burns down, your child needs an operation, a flood wipes out your business – you get it taken care of by public funding, at least enough to get you back on your feet. Sure, the system will need some fine tuning, but there are models in place around the world for at least health care and I don't see why it couldn't be extended to all kinds of adverse situations. A lot of the burden could be eased by a decent single tax system, where there would be some big deductible, say fifty or seventy five thousand, below which you don't pay any tax at all. Above it, a graded percentage kicks in, starting at maybe thirty percent."

Ed went on, "The important thing, though, is for the average citizen to have control over all the social benefits, with checks and balances in place to make sure the deadbeats who might like to abuse the system are exposed. The legislature and courts would go on as now, watching out to maintain a fair system. If they screw up, then there will be a simple way to boot them out of office. The big difference is the control would be more constant and powerful than it is now, where a legislator can be elected for years and do anything he wants to. And the insurance companies would be relegated to peddling insurance for automobiles and personal valuables."

"I don't know," Lyn said. "It seems to me it could end up with a greedy minority taking over, just like they are doing now."

"Let's hope not. The thing that encourages me is the way we live in a society governed by law. Law is good only as long as people believe in it. I'd think the same thing would happen when people are given the chance to control their own government. They would believe in it."

Lyn's words tempered Ed's certainty. He knew that even if the Reform Party assumed control, changes would not occur overnight. The popular support he was getting gave him courage to move forward with what he hoped would be a true and bloodless revolution. Still, he was too much of a realist to think that there would be no abuses by bands of opportunists. Sometimes doubts came to him in the middle of the night, but at the moment he just could not face the possibility of failure.

Those who were drawn to Ed Grendil to help him promote the Party were often surprised by the vitriol with which its platform was attacked by a well-heeled minority. The established political parties, funded and instructed by those who stood to increase their wealth under the existing system, spent huge amounts both on contrary advertising, in coercing the media to refuse RP advertising, and even in hiring hooligans to try to subvert RP gatherings. These methods merely solidified popular support. Within a year, polls indicated that a majority of voters were sympathetic, and the number rose daily.

The Grendil household had changed. Lyn and Ed had become much closer as the RP soared in popularity, in spite of great demands on his time. Besides reminding them of the idealism of their early days of protesting, the party activity was a substitute for previous family involvement. Carl had been gone for months, and they both thought of him only occasionally. Instead of the "business trips" that had occupied

Ed in earlier years, while the F-chip was under development, his absences now were to public affairs to address the volunteers. Lyn accompanied him sometimes, but mostly she stayed home to help draft new proposals for the party, and work with writers to incorporate them into the speeches Ed gave.

On a rare quiet evening together, they spoke of the children and simpler times. "I never expected things to go this way, did you, Lyn?"

"Who could have? It shows how much off the track the country has gotten since the second war. There's still an awful lot to be done, though, isn't there? Getting to the primary is just one thing, and it looks easy. What on earth will we do if you actually win the presidential election. There's such a machine of congressmen, senators, governors, and all that. Unless they go along, you won't be able to get much done, I'm afraid."

"You're such a pessimist," Ed said. "Even if I don't win this time, I expect that a lot of politicians will become Reform people after the election. It's going to shake up the system, I can tell you that. I expect some of our platform to be adopted, though it may take another election or two to swing the whole thing."

"I wonder sometimes about Carl. We haven't heard anything from him since he left. I worry about this military-like thing he's gone into."

"We didn't expect to hear much, did we? I don't think I'll learn much more than I know now about the SOS unless I get elected. You know as much as I do. From what we were told, it's very unlikely he will ever leave it. I'm not certain that he could, anyway."

"Then there are the twins," Lyn said. "We may as well not have had any children, for what we know of them. I still think it's kind of unnatural, those two living together all this time. I'm not talking about sexual things, just that neither one of them has ever had any interest in settling down with anyone else."

"Yeah, I've wondered about them, too. Maybe they'll come back and get involved in the party. We've sent them quite a bit of money. Maybe they'd like to pay some of it back." He laughed at this as if it were a preposterous idea.

Ed would have been surprised to learn that this very thought had occurred to Max and Anna. Their contributions to the life of the small town they had moved to had given them some purpose, but eventually Anna began thinking it was time to change their life again. The money Ed had faithfully given them for years seemed destined to continue, though they had read about how much he was putting into the Reform Party, and wondered whether one of these days even their modest stipends might come to an end.

For years Anna was willing and even pleased to be the family member closest to Max, who had an almost desperate need to attach himself to someone, an older or stronger person. For a while, Carl had shared this role with Anna, but now it was up to her. Whatever happened, she had resolved never to abandon Max, who seemed to be able to function only in her presence. Still, Anna and Max had started to feel some boredom and isolation in their lives. They knew of Carl's involvement with a super-secret quasi-military organization, and they of course knew of Ed and Lyn's involvement in the big reform movement. Everyone was doing something, except for them. They wondered whether they could somehow get in touch with Carl to try to form their close threesome once again, but they weren't sure how to go about it. They did remember Ed's old partner, Robert Sikes, and thought that perhaps he could help. They began trying ways on their own to contact him, with no luck until months later Max saw Sikes's name in a computer journal he sometimes read. The role Sikes had played in the early development of computers was mentioned, with some names and electronic addresses of a couple of people who had worked with him. Anna contacted one of them and got an address for Sikes in the tiny California town of Calamero. "You may not get any response," she was told, "but he does answer his email at least once in a while."

Anna wrote Robert Sikes, mentioning only that she was Ed Grendil's daughter, and that she and her brother Max might like to do something like what Carl had done. To Anna's great surprise, she got an immediate answer, and an invitation to come out for a visit if she and Max happened to be in the vicinity of Calamero. The town was on the northern California coast, and, though Anna could not have known, it was not more than a hundred miles from the Estate where Carl had gone.

Chapter 9
Mora

From his first days there, Carl reacted to every new experience at the Estate with enthusiasm, even the uncertainty of the long training session he was headed for. After his intense first day of initiation, he had several days at leisure to roam around the Estate, look in on training sessions in progress, visit the language libraries, and generally get acquainted. It was obvious to the SOS regulars that he was a new arrival and a little lost, just as they all had been when they first arrived. Often, a passer by would stop him and engage in conversation about some bit of trivia or humorous incident around the Estate. It helped put him at ease. The video in his room, and at various lounging spots around the Estate, offered a variety of informative programs. The broadcast by Jonas that he had seen in his rooms was directed only to him, or so he thought, but most programming was for everyone. He had no way of knowing that some of what passed as "news" was in fact fabricated to induce a stronger feeling of desire to participate in SOS problem solving. Carl was obsessively drawn to a video clip in which a tyrannical figure was having dozens of people executed in a most brutal way. Some of them were Americans. The tyrant was laughing with his associates, sipping a drink, during the slow and bloody death ritual. The announcer reiterated that there were still many dictators like this around the world, most of whom were dedicated to destroying the U.S. and its way of life. Carl wished he could confront and eliminate them then and there, and the idea of waiting months for training frustrated him.

Carl's training began in earnest a few days after his arrival. Part of each session was given over to orientation about the objectives and basic methods of the SOS. In his earlier life, at home with his parents, he had no idea how hated his country had become around the world, and how many leaders of other countries worked to undermine American influence, often planning terrorist attacks on crowded gatherings, or on the beloved icons of the country. Carl learned that his main job would be to take out the leaders of these subversive operations. He had been chosen to work inside the U.S., so he was not scheduled for the intensive language and cultural training given to many of the Soldiers. Instead, he concentrated on tactical methods and the identification of enemies. The lecturers were skilled, and they kept Carl's enthusiasm to serve at a high pitch. He felt the weeks go by quickly.

Each training day ended early enough to allow some leisure time and recreation for the Soldiers. Mora was in training for her next assignment, but she arranged her schedules so that she would run into Carl as often as possible. Whenever they could, they sat together for coffee, talking about many things other than their official training, though this was always at the back of their minds.

Once, a few weeks after his training had begun, she told him that soon she would be leaving on her mission, and that it would be hard for them to see each other afterward. "I've really enjoyed these times we've had together," she said. "I know it sounds Melodramatic, but we may never see each other again. Let's spend as much time as we can together. We're not supposed to get involved with each other that much, but, well, it's been. . ." Her voice choked, revealing an emotional side Carl had not known. He also felt drawn to her, and often had thought of the first moments when they had met.

The day was warm, and she suggested they spend part of the afternoon by the pool. He had fantasized about Mora sexually, but their relationship had always seemed too formal for anything more than fantasy, though now that much of his old shyness had dissipated with his training he began to think otherwise.

They lay together on a wide padded chair, sipping the ubiquitous colored beverage given to everyone all over the place. "Where do you think you'll be going?" Carl asked.

"I'm assigned to go to Cuba. My family's from there, so it's easy for me to learn the local accents. We've had people there for a long time, like my contact, who's been there for almost a year. Now it's time for me to do my part. But I probably shouldn't be telling you all this. It will be part of your training to see what we do in detail."

"Can you give me a clue? Mine will probably be quite different."

"I can say this much. I will be a reporter based in Guatemala, and my colleague will have arranged for me to have an interview with the President of Cuba. The regime is still terribly anti-American. Right now, their President has been successful in convincing all the hemisphere nations to cut off shipments of ethanol and oil to the U.S., and he would like to convince others in the rest of the world. He has a lot of influence, maybe because he started as a priest and can still make speeches that sway millions. What he preaches, of course, is to sabotage every American interest in South and Central America. After Castro died, everybody in Washington thought the country would turn around and become a U.S.-style democracy. But that didn't happen. The people there may not have liked everything about their socialist government, but they didn't want Cuba to become an American satellite. They elected another guy much like Castro, Raoul Sandro, who started out as a moderate, but became more and more anti-American as the U.S. politicians continued their pressuring and sanctions. So instead of reestablishing good political relations and economic trade, Cuba stayed on the U.S. black list. It's no surprise that Sandro continued the anti-American policies of Castro."

Though she couldn't bring herself to articulate it, Mora had doubts about condemning the Cuban government across the board. In the back of her mind were some nagging thoughts that maybe what Washington couldn't tolerate was a small communist country that had excellent health care, universal education, and a job for everyone.

She went on, "Anyway, he was much more effective than Castro was in converting people in other countries, mainly because of promotion of his splinter liberation theology program. He is apparently quite charismatic, and the anti-American movement would most likely collapse without him. That's where I come in. I won't say any more."

Carl knew there was much more to the assignment than that. He hadn't reached the point in his training where it was explained exactly how these problem people were dealt with, but he suspected it was something drastic and dangerous. He had already learned that assignments were to be completed, and that not coming back alive if necessary was part of the program, not that different from other Soldiers who go out to fight and face death. He could not imagine this happening to Mora.

"When do you think you might come back?," he asked. "I'd like it if we could get together again. I don't suppose there's any way we could communicate."

"No, that would be too dangerous to the secrecy of our operation. But I'll miss you, too, Carl. Let's just enjoy our time together now, and don't think about what may or may not happen. You'll see when you get your own assignment that you just never know."

She snuggled closer to him. He felt a surge of desire, though he wondered why she would want to spend the time she had before her departure with him, when she seemed to have so many closer friends among the Soldiers on the Estate. But these doubts evaporated when she raised her face and kissed him.

"Come to my place," she said. "We can listen to that music I told you about."

"This evening some time?"

"No, let's go now."

She got up, took his hand, and gently propelled him in the direction of her rooms. They were much like Carl's, though the interiors had oddly feminine touches, something that surprised Carl a little, since Mora seemed to be so dedicated to the SOS objectives. A small embroidered cat in an oversize frame hung over the faux fireplace, and small photos of her parents, or so he assumed, were framed in ornate twined wood frames on her dressing table. "Yours?" he asked, looking at the photos.

"My parents? Yes, in a way. I was adopted when I was eight, and they were good enough to care for me through high school, until I came here. I think they were glad when I left, but I have to be thankful for what they did."

Carl said, "Well, I lived with my biological parents, but I think they felt the same way about my leaving. My father seemed to know a little about this place, and gave me his blessing. Do you think you will ever go back home?"

"Oh, Carl," she said, "We find out at some point in our training that going back is not really an option for us. I think there's some fear that we have too many secrets. I don't know exactly, but I don't have any desire to go anywhere else right now."

By this time, they had moved toward her bed. They sat closely together, laughing a little when she had a little trouble helping him remove his clothes, or when he was unable to unclasp her brassiere. They embraced again, and she pulled off his shorts, briefly ran her hand over his enlarging erection, and tucked him into the bed. She went into the tiled bathing area to finish undressing, and came out to him beside the bed. She stood there for a moment, while Carl silently admired her body, which he thought, possibly from lack of experience, to be perfect beyond imagination. He vaguely recalled that when they first met he thought her facial features were ordinary. Now he seemed almost transfixed by them, and could not imagine anyone else to compare with her, much less having anyone else like her naked beside him in bed. She slipped under the covers and clasped him tightly. She could feel his aroused body, his erection, and it inflamed her to a spasm of excitement. She suddenly threw off the covers, and opened her body to Carl. He had only imagined this moment, and had never had any experience remotely like it to prepare him. But biology rarely comes up short, and some kind of hardwiring in his brain told Carl exactly what he had to do. He gently moved his hands over Mora's body, which was arching in anticipation, and she in turn brought his excitement to near climax with subtle movements of her hands. He would have liked to make their fiery penetration last forever, but biology again intervened and they soon reached their climaxes at almost the same time.

They lay quietly close together for a long time. Then they softly talked about what kind of future they might have together. It seemed utterly futile to try to plan for anything beyond the next few days. Mora opened up to him about her experiences so far. She had been in the SOS for nearly two years, and had completed two assignments successfully. One was minor, merely to provide some materiel backup to the two Soldiers who were actually carrying out the assignment. But for the other mission she was the principal actor, and carried the assignment to success with hardly a hitch. The target subject died within three weeks, and by then she was safely out of the country, although even had she been questioned, there would have been almost no way that suspicion could have fallen on her.

Carl hoped that he would have a record similar to hers before too long. Probably first a minor assignment, then one that tested all his abilities and training, with broad backup by the SOS. By now it had dawned on him that the chances of surviving more than a few assignments was small. There were no old SOS members that he could see; retirement did not seem to be in anyone's future. Oddly, the thought of dying while performing such noble service elated rather than depressed him.

Before he got up to leave, he thought of perhaps having sex one more time. But it seemed inappropriate after what had seemed to him the most perfect moment of his life. Instead, he dressed in Mora's bathing area, and she slipped on a robe. They hardly said a word as he gathered up a couple of things and prepared to leave. They were both overcome with the foreboding that this may be the only time they would ever have together.

"I'll come to where you are tomorrow," she said. "We won't be able to meet again like this, but it's something I will remember forever. It sounds a little shallow and old fashioned, because you and I hardly know each other, but I'm in love with you."

"Mora, this was my first time. I don't know what it would be like with anybody else, and I don't even know what it's like to be in love, but it has to be the way I feel right now, closer than I ever thought possible. We'll have to try to find a way to be together again somehow."

"We're in the SOS now, Carl. It's next to impossible. Let's just go our separate ways now and don't think about the future." She could hardly suppress the feeling that they were still re-enacting an old movie. "Let's just remember this wonderful moment."

Carl had dressed. There was little else they could say to each other.

"Goodbye, Mora."

"Bye, Carl, and good luck."

As he left Mora's rooms, he sensed he was being watched by a man standing quietly at the corner of the building. Carl moved toward him and said, "Hello, friend," a common greeting around the Estate.

"Hello. A little cooler now, isn't it?"

Carl wondered at the possible double meaning, but merely nodded agreement. In the heat of their encounter, both he and Mora had forgotten that they were both carrying F-chips and that their entire conversation was probably monitored. The thought had occurred to him briefly, but the last glass with the ubiquitous misamine still affected him, and the usual dreamlike state of tranquility once more dominated. He hadn't realized it, but one of the oddities of misamine had just been demonstrated. Its effectiveness greatly decreased in times of passion or other intense emotion.

Chapter 10
Training with Neurobots

Carl's later training was given over to filling in some of the details of SOS operations that had been glossed over in early lectures. He sat transfixed as the panorama unfolded. He learned of the multiethnic makeup of the Soldiers, who came from nearly every country in the world. Often they were from those countries that gave most trouble to U.S. policies. Although they spoke their original languages fluently, their SOS training helped them develop awareness of the importance of knowing regional accents. Further, regardless of the societal level they were born into, they were taught to handle themselves with no hesitation at any situation they might find themselves in, be it interacting with a working person or a king. Finally, the most important part of their training was learning how to work in a specialized profession such as journalism, acquiring enough expertise to practice it like an experienced pro.

After his brief grace period, Carl was immersed in full time mission training, and he had no time or inclination to reflect on Mora or anything else of a personal nature. After an extensive orientation, he heard detailed lectures on the advanced procedures the SOS had developed for canceling target subjects, a preferred euphemism for killing a victim. Methods to do this ranged from unimaginably high-tech neurobots to the crudest of suicide bombings. Fortunately, the high success record of the SOS had been won with only occasional use of unsophisticated methods. Neurobots had proved so useful that even the secondary backup methods of microbiological gene change had to be applied only occasionally. Nevertheless, Carl was expected to learn as much about each method as anyone in the SOS knew.

The development of neurobots had been spearheaded by Robert Sikes, though much of the detailed development was done by a cadre of young nanobiophysicists under his direction in the SOS laboratories near MIT. The latest designs were self-propelled bots about a hundredth as big as a red blood cell. Once introduced into the blood stream, they remain dormant until the blood passes into the brain, as all blood does eventually. Here in the most electrically active part of the body, the high concentration of neural activity produces localized electric fields, related to those producing brain waves. It is these electrical charge effects that are large enough for the bots to detect and be electrostatically drawn to. Once connected to neurons, the bots redirect themselves to a destruct mode, effectively beginning their intended function of disrupting certain neuronal pathways. The target subject gradually loses control over mental functions, slowly enough that the deterioration appears to be part of a natural process, some disease. By the time treatment is started, it is both useless and too late. The subject has already entered a one-way path toward brain death, with physical death coming shortly afterward. The whole process, when the initial number of neurobots is large enough, usually no more than a few dozen, takes only two or three weeks, accompanied sometimes by unbearably intense pain. Medical intervention has no benefit other than that gained by administration of numbing drugs.

Getting the few dozen neurobots unsuspectingly into the subject is the difficult part, and why SOS training needed to be so elaborate. There are several delivery options that range from infinitesimal darts that leave an imperceptible mark to devices designed to seek any moist orifice on the victim and quickly enter a blood vessel to discharge a cargo of neurobots, the delivery device self destructing afterward. These methods depend on the Soldier gaining physical access to the target subject, to be close enough for the transfer to be effective. By the time any symptoms appeared, the Soldier will have merged into the background, undetected, or at least such is the intention.

Typically, a Soldier would be chosen to become a reporter or a writer looking for an interview with the target subject. Mora Sanchez was trained to become a journalist in Cuba, working for a small publishing house in Guatemala. In an operation like this, the DI would usually set up a dummy publisher, and even print a few pamphlets sympathetic to the aims of the target subject. In this case the publisher actually existed, producing a newspaper called Tiempo de Fuego. The owner and publisher had been convinced that the interview to be scheduled for Mora was going to result in an important pro-Cuban piece that would improve his local image.

Mora's parents had emigrated to the U.S. from Cuba when she was six and had rarely spoken to her about political matters in either Cuba or the United States. They had wanted to blend in to the American culture and had succeeded, fitting easily into the community of Cuban expatriates living in Florida. Mora knew of course of their strident opposition to the Castro regime. They were bitterly disappointed when the Cuban people chose Raoul Sandro by a large majority and even more so when he turned out to support most of the ideas of Castro.

Mora herself was ambivalent about Sandro's politics. He had entered office through an election that was, at the time, considered fair even by U.S. observers. The people of Cuba clearly approved of his policies, so Mora had wondered whether the U.S. opposition to the Sandro government represented a hypocritical position that a democracy is only "good" when it agrees with American policy. Mora was young, strongly attached to an idealistic view that the people should decide their own government. If Sandro was their choice then the rest of the world should simply grin and bear it, open trade relations, and move on. Though she was too young to have paid much attention, she realized that this is what the U.S. policy should have been with Fidel Castro. Had trade relations been established, she thought, then Cuba would have long since been so economically bound up with America that earlier disagreements would have vanished.

Part of the indoctrination at SOS involved turning around any such preconceived beliefs that recruits brought with them. The U.S. had been a capitalistic society for generations, and the very idea of communism was anathema. Mora's early training at the Estate had been designed to change her simplistic view of communism from passive admiration to hatred. As far as anyone could tell, it had been successful. She was satisfied that the American Way of Life had been a positive driving force for the world for generations, and that it should be maintained at all costs.

Toward the end of her last month of training, she was called in to Thalia's office.

"Mora, I'm very pleased with the reports we have been getting on your progress. Would you mind if I asked a couple of questions?"

"Of course not. I'll be happy to answer anything."

"Yes. What I'd like to ask first is how you would feel if Raoul Sandro were to die in office, and be replaced by a more moderate leader who wanted to establish good relations with the U.S."

Mora was nonplussed by the simplicity of the question. All she had heard throughout her training was a catalogue of the evils of Sandro's government. "I would look on it as a first step toward a new and healthy government," she answered.

"You know that you were selected to go to Cuba and do just that, that is, see to it that Raoul dies in office, and fairly soon. Do you have any doubts?"

"No, I was told that would be my assignment. I'm ready to take it on."

"Good. Your assistant has been there for several months, and has a completely bland cover. You will be able to learn from him all the details about accessibility. You will go as a reporter for Tiempo de Fuego, a well established left-wing press in Guatemala City. You need some more training in idiomatic Guatemalan, quite a bit more on how to act the part of a journalist, and some updated training in the latest techniques we use to remove target subjects. You will of course be able to pass as a native Cuban if any difficulty arises. I think you will do very well.

"There is one other matter. We have a report of your seeing our new Soldier, Carl, in perhaps an intimate way."

"I thought it was just between the two of us."

"Mora, we need to know everything about our Soldiers. Intelligence isn't just about knowing about what others are doing in this country and overseas, it's also about knowing our own SOS members. Part of the reason is to give better direction."

"And the rest of the reason?"

"Well, if you must know, we are not pleased when our members become emotionally involved with each other. Sex is fine, it's something we all need. But if you fall in love, it's awkward. Love is an emotion that isn't compatible with our objectives of completing a mission, whether we live or die."

"I understand. I know I was carried away, and Carl was as well. But I plan to make sure that what happened between us will be just history."

"I hope so, or rather I expect it to be so. We cannot afford any weakness, emotional or otherwise, among our Soldiers, anything that could compromise a mission. Steps would have to be taken if it showed up." Thalia's throat felt dry as she finished with Mora. She liked both of these young people, and sympathized with their passion for each other.

"It will not. I am ready to continue my assignment." Mora, too, felt she was not being completely honest.

Mora's training took four more months, about the same time that Carl was being trained. When she had finished her term, she had learned complete details on how to deploy the latest neurobot devices. The part that made her uneasy was the implantation in her own body of counterbots to neutralize the attack bots should they enter her bloodstream, though she fully understood the necessity, since there was no true antidote. She also received chemical treatments to slow effects of the bots, as a backup precaution. She again worried about the consequences, but realized that being in the SOS required that one give up worries about safety. Successful completion of the mission was the only objective.

Carl and Mora had not seen each other during their training sessions for anything more than a hello or wave from a distance. Mora had gone through what would have seemed graduate training compared to the high school level Carl had experienced. But they were destined for quite different assignments. She was to leave within hours for her assignment, first to Guatemala and then to Cuba. When she saw Carl on the walkway, she asked him to have a coffee with her. They sat quietly, their feelings of desire and love returning, tempered with the sadness of parting.

"I guess you know by now, Carl, that these assignments we go on are often one way. Some never come back. We can hope, but probably it's best for us just to try to forget the days we had together. It won't help us get our work done. You know, we don't often spell it out, but SOS stands for Soldiers of Sacrifice. The idea is that we are ready to sacrifice ourselves to get the job done."

"Yes, I know that," Carl said. "I can do what is needed, but I don't have to forget about us – I know I'll have memories whether I want them or not. I'm just going to assume that somehow we'll be together again one of these days. It's not impossible."

"No, of course not. Just unlikely. Have you heard anything about your assignment?"

"Not a word yet. I think it will come in a week or so. The tendency is not to let the training get stale, I understand. Is there any way we could ever be in touch?"

"We have the communication implants, but I've never heard of anyone using them for personal uses. They're just for orders and emergencies, and even then only rarely."

"Who knows about all that?" Carl asked.

"I don't know him personally, but I was told it's Robert Sikes, the guy who invented a lot of that stuff."

"I know him. He was associated with my father."

"Small world. You would have to be the one who makes the contact. I wouldn't want to risk it. I can't do anything during my assignment that will look the least suspicious. Let's just see what happens."

They finished their coffee, and got up to leave. "Mora, just remember me."

"I will, Carl. Goodbye." Thalia's admonition about not falling in love flashed before her. She made the parting as impersonal as she could.

Within three hours Mora was on a plane to Guatemala. She chatted with a woman with two small children taking the same flight, on her way to Cuba. "My husband is already in Cuba," the woman said. "I'm not too happy about going, but at least we'll be together. I worry about him. He's selling Monopoly games over there. It's a good business."

Chapter 11
Sikes and the Reform Party

Ed and Lyn saw less and less of each other as the popularity of the Reform Party shot up to levels that were unheard of for any new third party. They still lived in their secluded and rustic house in Woodville, but with the explosion of interest in the RP, the town was no longer the backwater it became after its industrial base had failed years before. Lyn sometimes longed for those more uncluttered days, but she was committed to working for the party. Besides, its success had brought Ed much closer to her. It was as if he needed her personal closeness to calm him, and to offset emotional pressure from the throngs of well meaning strangers. What would happen later, and especially if her husband was actually elected president, she did not even consider. Others had weathered these monumental changes, and she could too.

She was elated when she received an email from Max and Anna stating that they wanted to come back to the area, if not to Woodville itself, at least to somewhere nearby. The reasons they gave were, as usual, vague, but she inferred from the mood of their messages that they were a little bored with their relatively indolent life. They did say that they would like to try to resume contact with Carl. Lyn had missed him more and more the longer he had been gone but had no idea that the twins felt the same way about him. Carl's gentle personality, his indifference to material wealth, and his dedication to the simplest of things endeared him to her, and probably to Max and Anna as well. She had no idea how she might help in reuniting the family but knew that it was a project she wanted to take on. She and Ed had mostly skirted the issue of Carl's involvement with the SOS, but she had become antagonistic and suspicious of it. Ed said that he wished he had not encouraged the initial contact of the SOS with Carl, though he still seemed to feel it was likely to be a good experience for him. The only intermediary Lyn knew between her and Ed to Carl's present situation was Robert Sikes. Since the day of the staged rape, she loathed Sikes in the way that one often comes to despise a person involved in a mutually despicable act. Entrapping Sikes and making a movie of it was one such act. Then, too, she had come to feel intense guilt about her first sexual encounter with Sikes that occurred just a short time before. She had enjoyed it then but now had deep regrets, especially after her relations with Ed had become so much warmer. Still, Robert Sikes remained her main hope in contacting Carl and perhaps getting him out of the secret group he was now bound up with.

In earlier years, both Ed Grendil and Robert Sikes shared equally high regard among the leaders of the administration for their work in developing the F-chip. Lately, however, as the Reform Party surged in popularity, Ed had become almost a pariah, though Robert's position was more secure than ever.

No one seemed to have an inkling about the deep unhappiness that pervaded the country when the RP began, or at least no one in the administration had taken the trouble to find out about problems at the grass root level. Some writers in the alternative presses had spoken of conditions being ripe for revolution, but even they said it was not a step to be considered until every other option had failed. And that had not quite happened yet. The RP landed in this climate of despair like a bombshell, with its advocacy of so many changes that affected the lives and welfare of so many people. The country was in a presidential election year, and Ed had placed his name on primary ballots around the country along with Alonzo White as Vice President. White was an old and trusted friend who thought much the way as Ed did on social problems. The voter turnout was nothing short of stunningly large.

The impact of this on administration officials was equally overwhelming. Suddenly, what had seemed to them a seamless political and industrial power bloc had been reduced to near minority significance. Emergency planning sessions were called constantly. The name of Ed Grendil became anathema. The confusion and anger filtered down to the DI, and, of course, to Robert Sikes. The President knew of his work and influence, and asked him to come to an off-the-record meeting. The two of them met in a small room at the White House.

"We only met briefly once before, Mr. Sikes. That was with the senior DI staff. I try not to interfere in their work. Any more than I have to. So I don't keep in touch very well. But I know of the tremendous service you have given our country. For many years."

"Thank you, sir. I think you know that my views are close to those of the administration. I have been happy to be of service to it."

"One thing puzzles me a little. I read in your file that you and Ed Grendil worked together some years ago. On a secret chip. Did you know him well?"

"Yes, though we were never friends. Even then, our political views were at odds. We got involved together in the chip design almost by accident, though we had very little to do with each other beyond conferring on technical matters."

"So you are not in touch with him now?"

"Not at all," Robert said. "We haven't spoken in a long time." He remembered the last time, smarting to recall Ed's snarling face as he burst in on him with Lyn.

"I'm looking for some ways to clip Ed Grendil's claws. We have to be careful. Our standing with the public is pretty low right now, if I'm reading the polls right. But it would be good to put some pressure on to get him to back out of the election. Or at least to reverse some of his insane platform planks. They would wreck the country. Or at least the business leaders. And our success as a power depends on business."

Robert Sikes was silent for a while. "It will take some careful planning. Ed Grendil is definitely a hard driver, and I have never heard of him being anything other than straight arrow. He has a son in the SOS, and two other children who've been living away from home. I don't know if any of them has any communication with Ed or his wife. Oddly enough, the two twins wrote me not long ago, to see if I could help them get in touch with Carl. I will be seeing them before long."

"I don't know what you might do with this kind of thing. You have my permission to try anything you want. Just be absolutely certain that it remains utterly top secret. But you wouldn't be in the DI if you didn't know that."

"Yes, sir. I will see what might be done. Shall I report back to you?"

"Only if you need some special help that the DI can't provide. Good luck."

"Thank you." Robert left the office, his mind turning over several schemes. He felt that Carl would be important in convincing Ed to modify his position, but Carl was not easy to access in his present situation, sequestered in training on the Estate. Interfering at this stage would not seem wise, and removing him altogether would defeat his future usefulness. He realized that Carl represented a valuable pawn in his plans to try to subvert Ed's campaign, though he would have to be careful. On the other hand, there were the twins, Max and Anna. They might be useful in applying some pressure on Ed and Lyn, and would be entirely expendable. .

Within a day of each other, he received two telephone calls at his house in Calamero, the first from Max and Anna and the next from Lyn. He made dates to see them on separate occasions. He felt sure he could come up with a plan to put pressure on Ed and perhaps cause him to withdraw from the primary, a plan that might perhaps also enable him to be with Lyn again. He had never forgotten the pleasure he had with her, partly because it was such a slap at Ed. He was embarrassed when Ed burst in on them, but later he relished the scene as being one of greater humiliation to Ed than to him. At least this is what he thought, little knowing about the security film that had been made of the event. He fantasized sometimes about convincing Lyn to leave Ed to come to live with him for a while.

As far as getting Ed out of the presidential race, there were several options he hadn't chosen to activate yet. It seemed a good idea to try the more benign ones first, as long as the President's wishes were carried out in a timely way. Robert Sikes was not a man of much principle, especially when it came to dealing with people he disliked.

He had asked Max and Anna to meet him at a San Francisco hotel, where anonymity of numbers would guard against prying eyes. They arrived midmorning on the appointed day and went up to his room. After an exchange of introductions, the twins gazed for a while on the sparkling bay scene spread before them from the wall of windows that made up one side of the room. Robert poured them drinks, and they sat to talk.

"I'm an old friend of Ed's," he began. "You haven't seen me in a long time, because for security reasons Ed and I were advised to remain separate as much as possible. You may know of our involvement some years ago in some devices that proved very useful to our country. In fact, you may have benefited from some of the money we made, which actually was quite a bit. It's because of our old friendship that I'm so concerned about Ed. I work for the Division of Intelligence, and I hear a lot of things about a lot of people. I recently heard some very disturbing news about Ed and his campaign with the Reform Party."

Anna said, "You know, Max and I haven't kept up very well with the various interests Ed has, not even with his new party. I do know it's been very successful. You're right about the money. We feel lucky not to have to worry about finances, but a lot of people in this country aren't. I guess that's why the party is so popular. Anyway, what did you hear?"

"This will no doubt surprise you. There are agencies that I have no control over who want him killed. His life and that of his wife will be almost certainly taken if he does not turn away from the aims of the party and try to defuse interest in it. You would be surprised to learn how many people with influence in this country and in the world feel threatened by his actions. The reason I wanted to talk to you was to see whether you could help in this diversion, for his sake, to save his and Lyn's lives. Knowing Ed, I'm sure that if we warned him directly, it would only make him more resolved to continue, and that would result in certain death for both of them. I would feel crushed if anything happened to them." His voice had become low, making his dissembling still more believable.

Anna and Max looked at each other, wondering what possible use they could be. They had not been close to Ed and Lyn for a long time, and in fact hadn't given them much time or thought beyond an occasional phone call or email. But the idea that their parents, their only parents, might be killed was disquieting indeed. Anna said, "We've been out of the loop, you know. I don't think we have much influence over them. It would seem very strange if we showed up and started asking them to renounce their party work, and his candidacy as president."

"Yes, I understand," Sikes said. "But there are other ways. I was wondering whether you would participate in a kind of game in which we pretend that you have been kidnapped and are in extreme danger. Your messages to Ed and Lyn would get their consideration more than anything I could say as an old friend, or that anyone else could say for that matter. Your ransom would be his resignation from the party. For the party's sake he would of course want the kidnapping and the negotiations to be kept entirely confidential. His resignation would logically be excused as the result of overwork. I'm confiding all this in you because, as I said, if I told Ed his life was in danger, it would only make him more resolute. I thought we might be able to convince him by other means."

The argument seemed to work. While they felt that the Reform Party represented something potentially good for many people, it did not seem to be something important enough to die for. They were unaware that Sikes had put a small dose of misamine in their drinks, just enough to blur decision making processes in favor of what was happening at the moment. "There's no danger to anyone?" asked Max.

"Not at all. You will be housed in a comfortable place while the negotiations go on. It shouldn't take long, I would guess."

"Well, let us think it over tonight. It seems ok. We'll call you tomorrow."

They got up to leave. There was more friendly hand shaking along with warm goodbyes.

"Until tomorrow morning, then," Robert Sikes said.

On the elevator Anna and Max stared blankly at each other for a while before pushing the down button. "I don't know what else we can do," Anna said. "I know we haven't been all that close to Ed and Lyn, but I would just feel like dying myself if something bad happened to them that we might be able to prevent."

"I feel the same way," Max said. "It's an odd thing to get mixed up in, a phony kidnapping, but Robert Sikes seems to have thought it out pretty well. We'll call him in the morning."

Robert got up early the next morning, anticipating their call. It came at eight. "We'll do it," Anna said. She spoke for both of them. "What do you want us to do?"

"We have to be careful to make the kidnapping look real. After lunch, say at one, the two of you could take a walk along the Embarcadero, staying a couple of blocks south of the Ferry Building. A car with concealed plates will come along, and you will be picked up at gunpoint."

"You said nobody would be hurt."

"Nobody. But it has to look like a kidnapping. We'll have a plant phone in the information to the police. Ed needs to know that there was a kidnapping in the city at the right time. You will be taken to a safe place south of town."

The mock kidnapping went off exactly as planned. As they walked, a car pulled up, two men got out, walked calmly to them, drew guns, and forced them into the back seat of the car. The tinted windows prevented anyone from looking in, but several passersby saw the incident. One woman screamed. The car sped off and vanished in the traffic.

Chapter 12
Kidnapped

One of the kidnappers introduced himself. "They call me Chilly. It's from some movie, I think. This is Augie. Another movie." The two men had put their guns away. "Don't worry about anything. If everything goes well, you won't have to be isolated for long."

"Where are we going?"

"It's probably safer that you don't know exactly the location. It's a kind of lodge. Very pretty. You'll be very comfortable."

The drive took about an hour. The lodge that Chilly had mentioned was in fact the very place that Mora used during Carl's recruitment into the SOS. It was still the same comfortable refuge, except that now Max and Anna were the guests and all access to the outside was secured. The two kidnappers brought them inside, showed them the kitchen with its well stocked refrigerators, the living room, and the bedrooms with spare clothing for both of them. The video machine did not receive broadcast channels, but there was a nearby stack of memory cards with hundreds of movies. Augie announced that he and Chilly would remain nearby, and showed them a call button to use in case of some emergency.

After Chilly and Augie left, Anna started to sniffle a bit. "I wish we hadn't got ourselves into this, Max. I think something terrible may happen."

Max, often more easily agitated than Anna, was now the calm one. "Well, I don't see anything to worry about yet. It's been just like Robert Sikes said, very low key. I can see why they don't want us wandering around, can't you?" Max took her hand.

"I hope it comes out right. All we have is Sikes's word to go on that there was no risk to Dad." Her voice was unsteady.

"Let's just wait a while and see what happens."

The news report that evening covered the kidnapping but revealed nothing about who was involved, or why. Although Ed and Lyn happened to be watching, they took no special interest in the incident. Shortly after the newscast ended, Robert Sikes called them to explain what had happened. He spoke first to Ed.

"I was asked to get in touch with you, since we are acquainted. The police are not involved, only the DI. You know kidnapping is a federal crime. We don't know who is behind this, but we do know what they want." He listened intently for clues from Ed to measure his reaction to the news.

"Money? We probably have enough to take care of it privately."

"No, it's more than that. They want you to drop out of the Reform Party and to make some statements about how you have had a change of heart about its mission."

"Sikes, I've never trusted you. Are you behind this?"

"Not at all. As I said, I'm the messenger. But I can tell you that they are serious. Something will happen to Max and Anna if you don't come through."

"Give us a little time to think all this over. How can we be sure they are ok now?"

"We talked to one of the kidnappers. They promised everything will be ok if you go along. That's all I can say. I wouldn't wait too long, say no later than tomorrow."

"We'll talk it over. Can we talk to the twins?"

"I don't know yet," Sikes said. "We're waiting for the next call. There's always another one. I'll ask then."

Ed said nothing for a long time. His mind was in turmoil, and he felt quite helpless. He first thought of making the event public, but felt it would bring chaos into their planning.

"Can I have a word with Lyn?" Sikes asked. Ed made a note of the phone number.

She had been listening to the conversation, with mounting apprehension. When she came on the phone, Sikes said some soothing words about being sorry, and sure that everything would come out all right. Ed heard her answers. What he did not hear was the next sentence Sikes said, "I want to talk to you alone. Come to the front of Angelou's Café at eight in the morning. I'll have a car there." He hung up.

She didn't tell Ed of her plans to meet Robert Sikes. What he wanted, she couldn't be sure. It could have something to do with releasing Anna and Max, or something to do with his lust for her, or both. Faithful as she was to Ed, she felt a little shiver thinking about Sikes again. In the rational part of her brain, she disliked him as much as Ed did, but they after all had been intimate.

Ed and Lyn talked for half an hour after the call from Sikes ended. Ed spoke about the children, and how important they had become in his and Lyn's lives. "You know, years ago I didn't want to have anything to do with Max and Anna, much less Carl. I feel very different now. I'm sorry we didn't try to bring them closer to us while they were at home. When this is over, that's what I want to do. Right now, I feel we should do whatever it takes to get them out. I'm sure Sikes has something to do with this, but it doesn't matter. Their lives may be in danger. As for the party, there are others who can lead it, maybe better than I would."

"This would be the biggest disappointment of your life, Ed, if you have to give up your work with the RP. Maybe there's another way out. Let's sleep on it tonight, and see in the morning. I'll need to go to town early for a few things, but I'll probably be back before you've finished breakfast."

Ed sat slouched in a soft leather chair as she left for bed. His mind raced with memories of the children, of Sikes, of his helping encourage Carl to get into the SOS, of whether all of this may be connected in some way. He dozed off in the chair and later groggily went to bed himself..

Promptly at eight, Lyn saw Robert Sikes in his car, walked to it and got in. He gave her a small kiss, squeezed her arm, and said, "How do you feel?"

"How would you feel if your children were kidnapped? If you had any, that is. Why did you want to see me?"

"Lyn, you know how I feel about you. I just hoped we might see each other again after this all blows over. And it will end quietly if you can make sure that Ed does the right thing."

"He wants to make sure the kids are safe," she said. "People are going to start asking a lot of questions if he changes his mind. The party is too big to walk away from now. I don't see how it could be kept secret, especially if word gets out about the kidnapping. It's all so confusing."

"Let me reassure you that it won't go any further than me," Sikes said. "I wasn't entirely honest when I told Ed I had nothing whatever to do with this. I had heard of it, and I might have some influence on the right people. What I'd like you to do is convince him that it's in the best national interests to shrink the Reform Party down as much as possible. It would be a long time anyway before it had enough strength to make legislative changes. It's better if the whole thing could be defused now, before too many people are involved. But the kidnapping was no joke. I must warn you that the lives of Max and Anna are definitely at stake."

"So you are behind this. I suppose I should have suspected. You have kidnapped my children, and right now all you want to do is make a date to get me to have sex again?"

"You're assuming too much, and making it sound so ugly. I just wanted to see you, and convince you to help out on the Ed matter."

"I'm going back home. I'll be talking to Ed again in a little while. We'll call you." Lyn realized that Sikes was a sick man and that further conversation with him might risk everything.

She got out without saying anything else. Robert felt a bit cheated. She had given him no hint of romantic interest on her part. Perhaps another time, he thought. He drove away, already thinking of the report he would make to the President. The effort had to be successful.

Chapter 13
Lyn

When Lyn returned home, she told Ed what had happened, especially the part that placed Sikes behind the scheme to have Ed renounce his interest in the Reform Party, and that Max and Anna could be in serious danger. She stopped short in her confessional about Sikes at telling him details of her first sexual encounter with Sikes, but brought up the second one.

"You know," she said, "We have the movie you took of that whole thing when you switched on the security camera."

"I know. He's trying a kind of blackmail scheme with us. Maybe it can work both ways."

"Let's be very careful, Ed. We don't know what they've done with Anna and Max."

"I'm thinking about that. I wonder if you should see Sikes again, maybe get him to tell more. If we had enough material to incriminate him, maybe the whole thing would die down."

"You're asking me to sleep with him again?"

"No, not exactly. Just entice him a bit, get him to loosen up, talk about some of the things he's doing. I can't think of any other way we could get him to open up."

Although she wouldn't admit it to Ed, the idea was oddly exciting to her. And for once, she would be doing it without the guilt. She agreed with the plan, making sure she didn't sound too enthusiastic. She called Sikes that evening.

"I thought we might get together again, Robert. Talk a little bit and then who knows what. Maybe I can convince you to do what you can to have Max and Anna released. We could discuss the other business about Ed's dropping out from the party."

This was not part of Sikes's plan. He didn't want to compromise his assignment to force Ed to resign. For one thing, failing in the objective would incur wrath from the President, not a pleasing prospect. Nevertheless, he didn't want to lose an opportunity with Lyn. Sex with her was an appealing thought, and perhaps she could after all help convince Ed to drop out. After a long pause, he replied, "That's a tough assignment, Lyn, but let's get together and see if we can work something out. I know one thing for sure, though, let's don't meet at your place."

She said she would drive up to his house at Calamero in the morning, getting there before noon. She and Ed spent an uneasy evening together, hardly talking, before going to bed. Ed was not prone to depression, but the complexity of life in recent weeks had drawn him down. Tonight was especially bad. He loved Lyn more now than he had ever realized, though with his involvement with the Reform Party he had almost no time to give to her. He felt sad when he sensed her isolation and loneliness, though she had seemed more upbeat lately as she helped with work on party affairs. The idea of her going to Robert Sikes was utterly repulsive to him, though with the stakes so high it seemed to be the only possible way to hedge their options. They went to bed, holding each other tightly for a while. Lyn, always liable to second thoughts, began to regret her plan to see Sikes. But she vowed to do what Ed had suggested, just entice him.

In the morning, Ed asked her to conceal a location transmitter in her car, and to wear earrings with a miniature recorder. As she drove up the coast she had no idea that the road would be passing only a couple of miles from the lodge where Max and Anna were confined. The scenic countryside cheered her somewhat, and by the time she reached Robert Sikes's house, she seemed to have mustered full resolve to carry off the encounter to her and Ed's benefit.

Sikes met her on the porch in a long robe. The day was already quite warm, and he invited her to change into something a little cooler. She returned wearing shorts with a thin tee shirt provocatively revealing the dark areolae of her nipples. He found her as alluring as ever. They sat on the porch, sipping drinks, without talking much at first. Lyn had switched on the recorder embedded in her earring.

"What would I have to do to get you to release Anna and Max?"

"I think you know the answer to that. All I can say is I can get the process started, and if you cooperate I'm sure we can all come to an agreement."

"I hope that it doesn't have anything to do with Ed's candidacy in the Reform Party. I hoped that when I came here that I could convince you to help get the twins released without Ed's having to do anything."

"Well, it isn't as simple as that, Lyn. I have some orders to carry out. I would be in serious trouble if I don't. I'd like to try for some intermediate plan, maybe getting Ed to ask his fellow party members just to delay things for a while. I don't know. I can't really promise anything."

"Who kidnapped Max and Anna?" Lyn asked.

"What makes you think I would know?"

"This is a political thing, Robert. Ordinary kidnappers wouldn't care about Ed and the party. You're an insider. You'd know about such things."

Sikes was visibly nervous. His eyes darted back and forth while he paused to find an answer. Lyn seemed primed for sex, and he didn't want to spoil the moment by arousing her suspicions.

"Well, I have to confess that I had a small part in the plan. I felt I was under orders."

"What part was that?" she asked.

"I talked to Anna and Max to convince them to play a voluntary part in the kidnapping. I told them that Ed, and maybe you, would be killed if they didn't."

Sikes stopped for a while. He was pale and shaken.

"I shouldn't have told you anything about this. My orders were to stop Ed any way I could. I came up with the kidnapping idea."

"I don't understand why you'd want to see me, much less tell me all these things," she said.

"I told you. I've wanted you more than anything since the last time. I thought that maybe you felt the same way. And I meant it when I said I would try to release your children, once we have some assurance from Ed."

"Who gave you your orders?"

"I can't tell you. Just that it's pretty high up."

"The President?"

He reached over and placed his hands on her breasts. "Don't ask any more questions."

She felt entirely turned off by Sikes. Still, she felt she had to get as much from him as possible, anything incriminating. She lay back, while he gently pulled off her shirt. Her breasts glistened from the warmth of the day. She pulled back. It was going too fast. She needed more information first.

"You know, Robert, if we're going to go any further we have to trust each other. I'm worried sick about Anna and Max, and I need to have some answers."

She leaned forward again. "So tell me, the President or what? I've got to know to fill in the picture. It's important to know how big the forces are behind all this."

Sikes was staring at her with growing desire. "Yes, it is the President," he said. "You can't imagine the pressure that he's under by the money powers in this country. The ideas of Ed's party would wreck the economy, lead to chaos."

Lyn knew that her visit to Sikes would not lead to any changes in his plan to have Ed drop out of the party as ransom for the release of her children. No matter what Sikes said, she would not believe it at this point, once she had learned what was behind the plan. She had already found Sikes utterly repulsive, but now things became difficult for her. If she turned him down cold, the fate of Max and Anna would be problematic. If she gave in to his sexual urge, he might or might not help get them released. Still, in view of the importance of Ed's withdrawal, it was unlikely they would be freed.

She sat naked before Sikes's gaze for a time almost more than she could stand. Sikes got up and paced a bit, clearly upset that he had been weak enough to tell her such revealing secrets. His own passion had subsided, replaced with a more cool headed consideration of what should be done about Lyn. She knew too much, and even if she deeply loved him, which he knew she did not, it would be too much of a risk to have her return to Ed. The idea of killing her was distressing to him, but he did not see any easy alternative at the moment.

Lyn could realize from Sikes's wild eyes and bobbing gestures what was going through his mind. It was a perilous moment for her. She tried to reassure him. "Would it be possible for me to give you my solemn word that I will never say anything about what you told me?"

Sikes heard something. He stopped and looked at her. "Put your shirt on," he said.

Before she could pull it on, a car drove up in front. Sikes went inside the house and emerged with a pistol. "I'll kill you first if you say anything," he said.

Ed Grendil got out of the car, and surveyed the scene for a minute or so. As he walked toward the house, Robert Sikes called out, "That's enough, Ed. What do you want?"

"I came to see if Lyn is all right," he said.

"She's fine, as you can see." Lyn had managed to get her shirt on and stood close to Ed. Sikes decided to play it as straight as he could. "We were just talking about how to get Anna and Max released."

Another car came up the driveway and parked behind Ed's and Lyn's cars. There were several people in it, but they did not get out.

"Just a few friends of mine," Ed said. "I thought we might run into car trouble."

Robert Sikes had placed the pistol on a table. What had started as a pleasant sexual meeting with a woman he lusted after seemed to be turning into a disaster. His only trump card was having Max and Anna under his control.

"Look, Ed," he said. "Let's try to go back a bit. I'll be sure to safely release your children immediately after you make a statement that you are pulling out as leader of the Reform Party. You know, the party will probably pick up the pieces later and someone else will take over. And your twins will be back home safe." Although he could say nothing more to Lyn, he assumed she understood the importance of silence. When the children were released it wouldn't matter what she said. All could be denied as the ravings of a distraught mother.

Lyn spoke up. "I have to tell you this, Robert. Our entire conversation out here is recorded on a chip in my earring. The whole thing."

"Good job, Lyn," Ed said. "And I also have news for you, Sikes. The film of your raping my wife shows the whole thing sharp and clear. You're a pretty big guy in the government these days. I wonder what these things would do for your reputation, not to speak of the President's. What do you think?"

Sikes frowned. Even in the corrupt political scene practiced now in Washington, these were not matters taken lightly, especially with his high position in the DI. The recording of his confession about the President was serious, but not as much as a filmed rape scene. The far right religious community that dominated much of the political system would have his head.

"Ed, I didn't think you had it in you. It was a good set up. I'm not afraid of my career. I have too much to offer those at the top for it to be in jeopardy. But why bother. Let's call the whole thing off. I'll see about having Anna and Max released right away." A nervous hoarseness to his voice betrayed the concern he felt.

"You will have to bring them safely home before we will release the recordings to you."

"It will be done by tomorrow."

Lyn went inside to change back into the clothes she had worn when she came. Ed and Robert sat glaring at each other. "We were a pretty good pair, Sikes. Funny how politics got in the way. I think we both have the interests of our country at heart. It's just that we come to them so differently."

Sikes made no effort to answer. Ed Grendil would have been dead by now if he hadn't had the foresight to bring backups for protection. But his time will come soon, Sikes thought. It will just happen differently.

Lyn returned and they went to their cars. Sikes sat on the porch until they left, his whole body shaking from the frustration and humiliation he had suffered once again from Ed Grendil. He vowed to himself to get revenge, then went inside to make a call to Thalia at the SOS Estate.

Chapter 14
Carl's Assignment

When he said goodbye to Mora, and in that last poignant moment as she boarded her plane to Guatemala, Carl felt a sense of desolation and sadness that he had never experienced before on parting with anyone. After he left home, it seemed the normal and natural thing to do, and he felt little emotion about it. He had a close feeling for Ed and Lyn as his parents and appreciated their providing for him, but leaving them gave him no anguish approaching what he felt at seeing Mora for possibly the last time.

He went to his rooms, started a file of music he knew she liked, and opened another can of fruit drink. He was aware that he could not resist the drink, but there was always plenty around, and he saw no harm in it. It calmed him and brought to mind some relevant parts of his training, the placing of duty to the SOS and the country before anything else, for example. Thoughts about Mora became suffused with his desires to succeed in whatever assignment he might be given.

He dozed a little but woke up when he heard a signal from his message unit. He looked at the reader, and saw it was from Thalia M'Gos. He knew it would be about his assignment. The message read, "Carl, please come to my office in the morning. I've got some news for you."

The training sessions for Carl had almost ended. He felt able to take any assignment he was likely to get, though in fact his training was not as extensive as many other Soldiers received. His skills were barely more than superficial compared to those needed by those taking advanced international assignments. He had learned little about journalism, interviewing, regional histories, languages and accents, technical improvisation, and a host of other topics essential to the needs of many of the trainees. Mora, for example, was able to take the point of view of Raoul Sandro on nearly any topic concerning Cuba, in a way that made her seem an engagingly bright and attractive acolyte to his cause. Furthermore, she had to know almost as much about the history and current situations of Guatemala, where her home publication was based. One of the benefits of misamine was its way of enabling sharp mental focus on topics important to the SOS community, so learning such massive amounts of material seemed almost effortless.

Carl sometimes felt he needed more training time to come to grips with some of the moral issues of the SOS objectives. He had never consciously hurt anyone or anything, even taking pains to avoid killing small insects or spiders. The idea of killing wasn't immoral to him, but he simply could not see any reason why life should be taken without reason. He had no power to produce life from nothing, so why should he be granted the luxury of taking it? The purpose of a military style training is, of course, to remove or cancel all such difficult questions from the minds of trainees, and replace them with an automatic response of obedience to orders, and perhaps even more important, replace them with a higher morality, based on the premise that the worst thing you can ever do is fail your fellows while you are carrying out your duties. This part of his training was made easier by the ever present misamine. One effect of this drug was the generation of a warmth toward his peers of the SOS, and deep concern for their well being. Still, in spite of the drugs he took, Carl had great difficulty in accepting the idea the he could take someone's life in the line of duty. It seemed reasonable enough to him intellectually, but when a reality modeling session brought it home to him graphically, he recoiled from the action of killing, even in simulation, and showed signs of becoming physically ill. His SOS trainers had encountered and convinced every kind of student, so Carl offered no particular problems, just a little more work. His reality modeling sessions showed steady improvement, and in the four months of his full-time training, he came to what seemed to be a complete turnaround.

After Ed and Lyn drove away from Sikes's house in Calamero, he had phoned Thalia to set up an urgent meeting on matters directly involving Carl. If there existed an SOS organization chart, she and Robert would be on approximately the same level. He was the technical guru behind many of the methods used by the SOS and other agencies within the DI, but she was in charge of actual training and maintaining the integrity of the SOS organization. The assignments of the SOS were not usually generated by either of them but came from very high levels in State. Thalia was responsible for their being carried out successfully, while Robert Sikes had to be sure that every technical innovation worked without a hitch, seamlessly hidden from everyone except the Soldiers directly involved.

Sikes went early the next morning to Thalia's office. He was always impressed by the Spartan way she kept the small room, with nothing unnecessary and everything in place. "Good to see you, Robert," she said. "We don't meet as often as we probably should." She had always been a little distant with him, never feeling comfortable with his mannerisms.

"That's true, Thalia. But I'm here on some urgent business. I've never called on you on anything involving the training and deployment of the SOS, but something terribly important has come up."

"Tell me about it, and I'll see what I can do," she said.

"It involves one of the current SOS, Carl Grendil. I would like to ask you to put him on a special assignment."

Thalia pushed her chair back and stared at him for a while. "You know where we get our orders, Robert. I don't see how I could do this."

"Let me lay it out bluntly. The President has asked me to find some way to get Ed Grendil to resign or otherwise leave the Reform Party. It has become a huge threat to the political, military, industrial, and religious leadership of this country. The President feels that if the party wins enough power, the country as we know it will be doomed. He told me to use any means possible to accomplish the mission and told me in so many words that he would not look kindly on anyone who put up a roadblock."

Thalia was surprised at the particulars of Sike's request, but she clearly understood what it might involve. She had been responsible for the removal of many people around the world who were considered troublesome to the objectives of the U.S. She had occasional misgivings, but on the whole she felt the overall loss of life was greatly reduced by the SOS methods. They had made the use of large scale military action nearly obsolete. Some of the removals had been people living within the American boundary who were considered subversive or potentially liable to engage in terrorist acts. But she had never dealt with a problem with such an urgent directive from top levels.

"This is quite a request. You know how easily things could go wrong. I suppose I would be the one blamed if the mission fails?"

"He wants the job to be done. I would expect everyone who helps it succeed would be rewarded with his thanks, if nothing else. If it fails, well, I don't know. I will make sure you remain anonymous in that case."

She didn't believe him, and even suspected that he would say anything that came into his mind to protect himself. Still, her choices were limited. "What do you want me to do?" she asked.

"I know that Carl Grendil has just finished his training for work within the country. I want you to assign him to kill Ed Grendil and his wife Lyn, or cancel them out as target subjects, whatever you like to call it nowadays. There may be other work to be done later, but the belief is that by stopping them the party would collapse."

Thalia was taken by surprise. It was some time before she could respond. She had come to like Carl, at least all that she knew of him. Besides that, she had never had to deal with any assignment that had such a personal aspect.

"I don't know about the politics, but I've never been involved in something like this. You must know that Ed is Carl's father. It seems to me to be a bad idea to have Carl involved. There are family relationships that might make it extremely difficult for him to carry out the assignment."

"It is unusual, I have to say," said Sikes. "But logistically it is the most appropriate assignment I can think of. Carl would have easy access, he has all the methodology to implant the brain seeking bots without detection, and could easily return safely to monitor the results without fear that his involvement would be learned."

Thalia had no idea of the venomous hatred that Sikes harbored for the Grendils, so he seemed to her to be merely laying out a logical plan. She was not given to making deep moral judgments, and she could not see any way to counter his reasonable argument. After a long pause, she agreed with his proposal.

"The logistical part makes sense," she said. " I dislike the idea, but it might work. We will have to make sure that Carl is well medicated, and understands what he will be required to do. I suppose the plan will work, but I still wonder why we don't have some more neutral soldier trained to do this."

"Time is short, Thalia. It would take too long to get someone else."

"I will speak to Carl about his assignment."

"Thank you, Thalia. Let's keep this to ourselves for the moment."

Chapter 15
Homecoming

Ed and Lyn came back to their house after a long and quiet ride, filled with doubts about what might happen to Max and Anna. Robert Sikes had been cornered, and although he agreed to release them, he could not be trusted. Their own private rooms were dark and damp when they returned, and their first thoughts were to brighten them up with light and heat. After an hour or so, they began to relax a little and look optimistically on the return of the twins, though their sleep later that night was fitful.

Early the next morning the familiar black car with dark-suited driver drove into the driveway and left Max at the doorway, with no baggage. He knocked on the door. Ed was in the kitchen, making breakfast. When he came to the door, he greeted Max with a feeble smile and finally a perfunctory hug. There was a long pause, and then, with a long face, he greeted Max with the question, "Where's Anna?"

"They kept her there," Max said. "I think they want you to give up some things before she will be released. They did say that to go to the civil authorities would jeopardize her life."

"That's probably true at this point," Ed said. "I know the bastard behind all this. He could hide under his DI cloak and avoid anything the police could come up with. And it would not be good for Anna. What's your story about the kidnapping. Sikes told us it was arranged."

Max said, "Yes, it was just that. But after we agreed to it and went off to some kind of lodge hidden in the woods, I got worried. After a few days, I was convinced we would never get out of there alive. All we had was Sikes's word. I don't know why we ever got mixed up with it. Sikes said that something terrible would happen to you if we didn't help force you out of your party. While we were being held, we got the idea that we were all going to be killed anyway. It really freaked us out."

"How do you think Anna will manage there?" Ed asked.

"I don't know anymore. We never saw Sikes again, only these two guys who brought us there. They didn't seem especially violent or mean. But with her there by herself, I don't know."

"I was worried about you and Anna all along," Ed said, "especially when I found out that Sikes was the contact. It seemed very odd to me. He's obviously being pressured to have me drop out of my party activities. Politics is bad enough if you're just looking on from the outside, but it's really shitty if you're in the middle of it."

Lyn had come into the kitchen, and Ed gave her a summary of what had happened. She sat quietly. Sikes had told her of the President's involvement, but she thought it might be best to keep still about it for the moment. She had hoped that everything would blow over when the twins were released. Now with Anna prisoner, and Carl still under the SOS control, she realized that the whole situation called for extreme care if they were to be seen again. Telling Ed what Sikes had told her about the President would only complicate matters, to no purpose that she could see.

She finally said, "The first thing is to get Anna back. Then we have to get Carl back home. I don't like his being in this SOS thing, almost like a prisoner as far as I can see. I don't know much about it, but I do know that Sikes has something to do with getting him involved in it."

"He's the technical guru for SOS," Ed said. "I still don't know much about the organization either, but I do know that the members are trained for special assignments all around the world. You may not remember Bob Smith, the contact I had that convinced me it would be a good thing for Carl to join the SOS. We've talked a couple of times since and I found out a little more. The SOS is trained to get close to troublesome leaders anywhere and take them out. If things go well, the Soldier gets away long before something happens to the victim. If they don't then they are expected to die without revealing anything, or to kill themselves in an attempt to complete the mission. Apparently quite a few get back, but not all."

"Let's get Anna back, then get Carl out of there," Lyn said. "We've got to find a way somehow."

"Sikes may be our best hope for everything, unfortunately. We do still have the movie and the earring chip. They won't help with Carl, but at least we can trade them for Anna. We'll have to use some other way for Carl. I'll have to try to find out more about the SOS, where they are located, someone to contact. When Bob Smith got his information about the group, most of it came from a woman named Helen McLear, who is close to the SOS director. I do have the last number Sikes called us from. I'll start from that. It's his house in Calamero."

He was a little surprised when Sikes answered with just "Hello."

Without any preliminaries, Ed said, "I have the video and chip. How do you want to do the transfer. I will have to have Anna safely in my custody before you get the material."

"Fuck that stuff. I don't care what you do with it. But I am keeping Anna with me until I am sure you make some public announcement about leaving the Reform Party. I want to see the thing collapse."

"You want to see the party collapse? What do you care about the party? Who's paying you."

"Nobody." Sikes was surprised Lyn hadn't told him. Perhaps she did feel something for him after all.

"I don't think my renouncing the party will make that much difference to its success. There are millions of people supporting it now. They'll just select someone else to carry on."

"Well, we'll see. Do it anyway if you want your daughter back. She's quite pretty, isn't she?"

Ed ground his teeth. "Sikes, if anything happens to her, I swear I will kill you personally."

"Nothing will happen to her if you write your resignation, and give some convincing reasons why you are turning against the Reform Party."

"I'll call you as soon as I can." He knew, though, that he would not give in to Sikes.

"No, I'll call you," Sikes said. "I'm moving to another location with a different communications terminal."

Ed hung up and sat silently for a long time. Lyn came to sit beside him. She put her arm around him "It's become a mess all of a sudden, hasn't it. A short time back we thought the kids were safe somewhere. Now they all seem to be in the thick of some kind of trouble. I wish we knew more about the SOS thing, then maybe we could help get Carl back."

"We'll all be together one day. I just have to think things out. I know Sikes, and his habits. He's the only one that can help at this stage, I'm sorry to say. We'll get him to help, and we'll get him, one way or another."

Chapter 16
Carl

When Thalia met with Carl to give him his new assignment, she made sure that he was deeply under the influence of misamine. The procedure she was carrying out was unusual to say the least. First, it came directly from Robert Sikes instead of through normal channels, but more upsetting to her was the assignment itself of having a son kill his own father. She was too much of a soldier herself not to carry out orders she felt had come directly from the President, but it was shaking her faith in the system. If anything went wrong, she was certain she would be blamed for it, though she felt sure she would make Sikes's involvement known. They would both probably feel the wrath of the DI.

The amount of the drug in Carl's drink, when they sat in her office, was much larger than usual. The effects were noticeable. He was alert and able to communicate normally, but there was an unnatural intensity in the way he focused on her words, as though each was being burned into his brain. Thalia made a few conciliatory remarks, then carefully formulated her official description of his orders.

"Carl," she began, "We are proud of our Soldiers and what they have accomplished already, as well as what we expect of them in the future. With very minor exceptions, they have never failed us. I know that you have completed your training, and are ready for an assignment yourself. There is one that you can carry out more easily than anyone else. It may seem difficult to you, but I have every confidence in you. It should not take you very long at all."

"Thank you, Thalia," Carl said. "Being in SOS has made me feel part of a group in a way that I have never experienced before. We all feel that the mission of one of us is a mission by us all, and that failing at a mission and disappointing our fellow Soldiers is just something we won't tolerate." His words seemed to come out mechanically, but in fact he meant them.

"Good. I have written out your mission in an official way. Read it, remember it, and destroy the paper. You can begin as soon as you are ready." She handed a folded slip to Carl. The notice, printed in a small but easily read typeface, read

Soldier Carl,

This will be your first mission. Congratulations. You should first check into stores to receive updated equipment, then proceed in a timely manner to the residence of target subject Ed Grendil, in Woodville, California. By the procedures in which you have been trained, you will take the necessary steps to cancel the subject. After completion of the mission, you will report back to the Estate. You must be aware that if the mission fails, you must face the usual consequences. I do not believe that you will fail.

Success be with you

Thalia

The full significance of the message did not register instantly, though at no time did Carl have any doubt of carrying it out. He was aware that he was being asked to cancel a target subject, this time his own father. He was strangely remote from any personal feelings about the act. Under the influence of misamine, the assignment burned itself into his brain much as Thalia's initial remarks had. While he felt it must be an unusual assignment, to be asked to cancel a subject so closely related, he was trained to accept the fact that the act of canceling was merely an act of duty, with no moral or ethical taint involved. He looked up at Thalia, and gave back the note. She placed it into a liquidation box.

"I understand the assignment, and I assume it has to be done this way. OK. Is there anything else?"

She looked at him as if searching for hidden emotions. "No," she said. "You may begin immediately. As the note says, success be with you."

She stood up, and saw Carl out. She rarely felt any emotion about those who were targeted, but this time she had tears in her eyes. She wished she could have turned Sikes down, but she was too much a creature of the military mind to contemplate any alternative.

Carl stood on her step outside the building, briefly looking up toward the bright sun. He cast a glance at the walkway before him, where a few straggling weeds struggled through cracks in the pavement. He went to his rooms, tried to relax for a while with music, and awaited the next stage of his mission.

He was to be driven to his destination in the black limousine. Since he was returning to the house he had once lived in, he needed to take very little with him. His arsenal of neurobots and self-destruct equipment had already been prepared and was waiting for him as he left the Estate. He made sure the delivery system was concealed, packed a couple of small items, and was ready to go. When he looked outside, a driver was already waiting for him.

On the way back to Woodville, thoughts of home and his previous life flitted before him, though in very abstracted vignettes, far removed from coherent memories. He thought of Ed, his father, the target, only in terms of an image that he must recognize in order to carry out the mission. What was the mission for? He had no idea and would not ask. Maybe when he returned he would find out. Often, after especially difficult missions, a Soldier would be accorded a ceremony of special recognition, at which the reason for the mission might be revealed.

The driver did not speak. Carl asked him if he had been here before. "Yes, quite a while back. I was here a couple of times. Nice area."

Carl asked him to let him off some distance from Ed's house. A convenient place was the Zone, where he had first met Mora. It was not very far from the house, and would make his return seem quite natural. The driver knew where it was. "This is where I came before," he said.

Carl got out, and the limousine slowly moved away. The place was deserted, just as it always had been, and quiet, just as always. The sun was warm, and when Carl walked for a while, he felt sweat on his brow. He walked very slowly and could not help but notice the light and dark shadow patterns. He had encountered nothing like this since he had left home many months ago, and their recognition was almost like discovery anew. He stopped at a stone bench, a place that seemed very familiar, and sat for a while. Walking slowly, old memories returned, memories of light and shadow patterns he had seen before on wooded walks and here in the industrial desolation. He remembered first seeing Mora. He was confused. The assignment came first, and here he was being distracted. He went on toward the house.

He stood at the door for a long time before pushing the doorbell. A man helping with party work came to the door. Carl had never seen him before. "Yes?" the man asked.

"I'm Carl Grendil. I've come back home. Is my father here?"

The man did not recognize him at once and regarded him with some suspicion. But apparently he eventually recalled seeing Carl's picture in the house somewhere. "Yes, he's here," he said. "Come on in."

Carl went into the kitchen area, the familiar place for meeting, and sat by the table. After a few minutes, Ed came in. He wanted to greet Carl with a hug, but Carl hung back. There would be time later. "Hello, Dad. Are you ok?"

"Reasonably well, Carl. It's good to have you back home. They told us when you enlisted in the SOS that we might never see you again. Lyn and I have been worrying about you. Has something happened?" Ed could sense that Carl was not the same person he once was.

"No, not at all. I finished my training, and I have an assignment to carry out."

He looked at Ed. The confusion in his mind grew. The patterns of light and shadow he had just seen again seemed to take control of his brain. It was as though the images were competing with the misamine, almost canceling its effect. The determination he had felt about the assignment did not seem so strong. Nevertheless, he felt compelled to complete it. He stood up and went toward Ed.

They shook hands and embraced in a half hug. Carl was in a perfect position to transfer the packet of neurobots into Ed's body, with no chance whatever of detection and complete ease of escape. Carl did nothing. His seemed to be regaining some control over his mind and losing some of the influence of misamine. The impact of the memories he had just experienced outside, and now with his father, seemed to have at least partially canceled the drugs he had been taking.

"Dad . . ." he began. "I. . ." His words faltered. He put his head on Ed's shoulder and began to weep. "Dad, I came here to kill you."

Ed pulled back, looking Carl closely in the eyes. "What are you talking about, Carl? What's going on?"

"It's my assignment. I thought it was proper to do it. I have these tiny weapons that infect the brain. You would be dead in a few weeks. Nobody would ever know how it happened. I couldn't do it. Something changed me on the walk over here."

"Come over here and sit."

Carl bent over, his head in his hands. He was beginning to feel the need to take one of the misamine capsules, beginning the early stage of withdrawal from the alkaloid they contained. "Dad, I'll need some help with this. I need the pills."

"What is it?" Ed asked. "Did they give you some sort of addictive drug?"

"I don't know. I think so. They never tell us the details of the treatments we get. But that's what everybody seems to think. They call the main drug we take misamine, and probably the idea is to keep us taking it regularly. I'm beginning to feel it now." From his training, Carl knew of the drugs all the soldiers took but had never thought of them in any way other than as something that made him feel warm and close to comrades.

Ed went to his medicine bag and brought out some small tablets. "Here, take one of these," he told Carl. Carl swallowed it and after ten minutes or so seemed more calm.

"What is that?" he asked. "I feel a little better."

"That's what I needed to know. I guessed right. Take two more."

In an hour Carl's agitation had vanished, and while he still seemed a little stupefied, he could speak rationally.

"It's a whole drug culture there. They give us something with every bit of food or drink we get, plus all sorts of pills that are required. I had no idea what any of them did. It was impossible to stop taking them."

"Don't be concerned now, Carl," Ed said. "I keep some of these alkaloid receptor suppressors around. They work with quite a few addictive drugs. They seem to be working with this one. Let's just keep up the treatment. After a few days you won't need them at all."

After a night of fitful sleeplessness, Carl woke with a clear head, and a feeling that he may be escaping the effects of the misamine. The intense pressure of having to feel a part of a close knit group was vanishing. He was able to sense some of the feelings he had before entering the SOS. When he went to breakfast, Ed and Lyn were already in the kitchen, puttering with breakfast things.

Lyn was torn with emotions. She was overjoyed to have Carl back home, vowing to herself that from now on it would be a functioning home, not the hangout of near strangers that it had become when the party work began. On the other hand, she was sick about the continued confinement of Anna, now still under the control of Robert Sikes. She felt that somehow she was to blame for the kidnapping, that her involvement with Sikes, and her rejection of him, all had made him determined to destroy the Grendils.

They sat at the table and began to try to plan for Anna's release. Lyn said, "I don't want to make too much of this, but you know that Robert Sikes has occasionally been strongly attracted to me. Maybe I still have some influence over him, enough to see him again and try to get him to release Anna."

More intensely now, Ed felt some of the jealousy he had experienced before when he sensed that Lyn's involvement with Sikes had given her more pleasure than she let on. He knew only of the time when they set Sikes up in the simulated rape scene. She had hinted at others. He did not want to know details. "What do you think you could do?"

"I can call to meet him," she said. "I'll try to talk him into going back to the way things were. If that fails, I will try to kill him."

Carl spoke up, "That doesn't make sense. If he's dead, we'll never find Anna. That's a really bad idea."

"He'll be much more cagey after the last time, when we brought our guards along," Ed said. "It may not go well at all for Anna if he feels trapped. And definitely not well for you." He began to think Anna's rescue seemed hopeless.

Carl said, "There is a possibility. I do have the collection of miniaturized neurobot weapons I was issued when I came here. Perhaps I could meet with Sikes."

"He'd never do it," Ed said. "As far as he knows now, I will be dead in a few weeks by your hand. He knows what you're capable of and won't take any chances that you might turn on him."

Lyn interrupted, "He couldn't know anything like that about me. Carl, show me how to use those things, and I will go to him myself. I have an idea."

Ed and Carl stared at her as though the plan seemed insane, but finally they both realized it might be the only way. "I can teach you in a few hours," Carl said. "One thing is very important. Sikes needs to think that I carried out the mission successfully and that I've returned to the SOS Estate."

"I'll know what to say. You can start teaching me the methods after I call him."

She still had the private phone number he had given her long before at their first encounter. She called and got a robotic sounding voice mail. In the most innocent sounding voice she could manage, she asked for Sikes to call her.

"Let me talk to him alone when he calls," Lyn told the family.

Ed agreed. Whether he liked it or not, Lyn was probably the only person close enough to Sikes to make any kind of plan work. If she could get Sikes to release Anna, then maybe he should stay out of it for the time being.

It was another two days before Robert Sikes called. Lyn answered, and took the call in another room. "I wanted to talk to you. I don't think you and Ed can ever understand each other well enough to get anywhere with this standoff. Where can we meet?"

"You tricked me last time with the earring signaling device, having Ed follow you to my house, and all that shit. I'm not going to risk that again." Recent events had clouded his already deranged mind, and he was having trouble thinking clearly about what had happened, but he seemed drawn toward seeing Lyn once more. Perhaps it was just the idea of getting at Ed by dominating her. It still seemed to make sense to him.

"There won't be anything like that. You have Anna and I want her back."

"Drive to Santa Rosa, and when you get there I will call you and give you directions. I swear that if you are followed, or tell anyone where you are going, I will kill you and Anna both."

"I will be completely alone this time. It will take me an hour to get there."

She thought of what she was getting into during the drive to Santa Rosa. When she was almost there, her phone rang. Sikes gave her explicit directions, and within another hour, she was at the lodge. Though Lyn was unaware of it, Anna was still there, since Sikes thought that moving her would expose him to risk. She was secluded in a soundproof room at the back of the building, but of course Lyn had no idea where she was. When Lyn arrived, Sikes was already there, parked in front. They greeted each other in a diffident way.

She began, "Ed is a pretty stubborn man, Robert. I don't think you realize how difficult it would be for him to give in to you over this Reform Party matter. If you kill Anna, or even hurt her in any way, he would use every resource he has to get you. But I have some influence over him."

"I don't see how. You never seemed very close to me."

"That was then. It's different. If you release Anna, I will convince him to drop out of the party, and even publish reasons why he's doing it."

"If I assume you are telling the truth, what guarantee do I have?"

"I will stay here with you. As long as you want me."

With Ed out of the way, as Sikes believed he would be in a few weeks if Carl had done his job, he had no further reason for keeping Anna, and his interest in Lyn had faded to nothing more than momentary lust. Unfortunately for both of them, they were far too aware of his part in the kidnapping to let either of them go free.

"What went on at your house before you called me?" he asked.

"The big news was that we saw Carl again. Max is at home safely. We hope Carl can come back to us too."

"Oh, yes. Carl. A little family reunion."

"I was so happy," she said. "Carl said he was just on a short leave and had to return to start another mission. He only stayed a couple of hours."

"How did he and Ed get on? SOS people don't usually come back home."

"They were never very close, but they talked for quite a while. And when Carl left, he hugged Ed for a long time. I'd never seen him do anything like that before."

Robert Sikes seemed to relax from the formality he had maintained so far. "Yes, it's good he came home. With the missions they go on, it's always risky." He was convinced that this mission had been carried out successfully. In a short while, the President would learn that the leader of the Reform Party had died. His last hurdle was what to do about Anna and Lyn. He knew he had to keep at least one as hostage. Letting both go would be dangerous for him, though his thoughts about what might happen were becoming muddled.

He told Lyn, "I have decided to let you go. But I will keep your daughter here. If you treat me well, she will be safe. Otherwise she won't be."

"Treat you well in what way?" she asked.

"One more time together," he said. "With the videophone showing us to Ed, together." Lyn knew of the hatred that Sikes felt toward Ed, but had no direct experience of it before. Sikes, whose mind seemed more and more unhinged, smiled almost like a villain in an old melodrama. To him, this would be his final revenge, a memory of shame that Ed could take to his grave.

Lyn was not surprised at Sikes's proposal. His perverse mind had amply revealed itself to her before. She listened calmly. She knew what she had to do. She had dressed with a thin top, and wore a skirt with no underwear.

"That's pretty wild, Robert. I'll do it for Anna's sake, but let's get ready before you call Ed."

She unbuttoned her shirt, her still youthful breasts pushing against a translucent bra. Sikes's interest in her, temporarily dormant, once more came alive and he began to lose control. She moved closer to him, grasped his waist and pulled him toward her. As he reached between her legs, groping for her naked crotch, she unleashed the full charge of neurobots into his body. He seemed to feel nothing. She pulled back, and buttoned her shirt.

"What are you doing?" he asked.

"That's it for you, Robert. I got the neurobots from Carl. You will be dead in a few weeks."

"What the fuck are you doing. I'll kill you both right now." He was almost in shock. He stumbled toward a night stand to get a gun.

"I had to, Robert. I think you're turning into some kind of animal. But I have a trade off. I can get you an antidote. They developed it just before Carl came to visit us." She had thought of this story back at home while she planned her visit to Sikes's house. She didn't know whether there was an antidote or not, but neither did Sikes.

"You bitch. You've really fucked me over, haven't you?"

"I'm just trying to keep my family in one piece."

"Family? What about Ed? Didn't Carl kill him. Were you lying about that, too?"

"No, he didn't" she said.

"Shit! So he didn't kill Ed after all. I"ll have to do it myself. I'm still under orders of the President." This was just babble on Sikes's part. In fact, the President's orders were of little interest to him just now. He wanted to save his own life. He could worry about orders later. Nothing else mattered. Least of all Ed, Anna and Max, or even Lyn.

"If you want to live, you must release Anna, and let us go home peacefully. Carl is the only one with the antidote. When he gives it to you, you will live. If you kill us, then you will die as well. It's your call."

"I don't trust any of you, but I don't have much of a choice now, do I? How would I get it?"

"Carl will come here with it tomorrow. You will have to do exactly as he says."

Sikes, by now acting almost robotically, went to the back of the lodge to unlock Anna's door. She came out, looking haggard and unkempt. She briefly hugged Lyn, and they both walked to the car without looking back or speaking, leaving Sikes alone staring distractedly after them. He could no longer think clearly. He thought the neurobots were destroying his brain already, though actually it might take a few weeks. Perhaps this was a newer version. He could only guess, and worry.

He had purposely been kept away from some of the latest DI developments, since many who had known him for a while had become aware of his increasing paranoia and irrational hatreds. One important quality needed for someone carrying DI secrets is the ability to maintain an emotional stonewall. Mental weaknesses of any kind could breach security. In Sikes's case, because of his useful service in the past, he was kept on the payroll, though denied access to any late developments.

He detested the idea of having to rely on Lyn to carry through with her promise, and at bottom he doubted that she would. Still, it was one option, maybe the only one. The other was to go directly to Thalia and get the antidote from her, assuming she had it and would give it to him. This was a questionable option, too, but it would be the only one in case he got nothing from Carl. His sleep that night was filled with nightmarish visions of an agonizing death.

Chapter 17
Mora's Mission

On Mora's flight to Guatemala City, she used some of the time to review her skills in Cuban history and language. Most important, however, was her mental review of the various ways of introducing neurobots into her target subject. It was her first mission to take out someone herself, and the importance of it was just sinking in. Raoul Sandro was, after all, the president of Cuba, not just some minor thorn in the side of the U.S. She never questioned the motives of missions, nor did any other SOS member after they had become part of the close knit group. She did wonder what effect the removal of one person might have on an entire movement, or indeed the whole country, but the prevailing belief was that it avoided need of further military action. The confusion of establishing another leadership, with all the painfully slow development of trust and obedience, would effectively erase any belligerent motives for a while, perhaps indefinitely. In the meantime, the U.S. would act as "good cop" for a change, giving the country a chance to become part of the American dream instead of remaining a renegade. At least, this was the theory. Once in a while it worked, though more often not.

The office of Tiempo de Fuego could be described fairly as a hole in the wall. The staff included the editor, a secretary, two reporters, and a general factotum who prepared the copy and took it to the printer. Even so, it had gained considerable respect in Central America, and was regarded as the leading left wing voice. The paper depended on volunteer reporters like Mora, and she had brought along excellent if fabricated recommendations from small left wing papers in the U.S. The staff of Tiempo de Fuego would have been stunned to learn of her motivations, but there was no reason for suspicion. She fitted in perfectly from the beginning of her stay, assuming the role of visiting reporter with grace and skill. In the few days before she left for Cuba, she wrote a short article about the leftist party in Guatemala that the editor included in the next issue. He was reassured that her visit to Cuba would produce several articles about Sandro that would be outstanding.

Mora spent her spare time wandering around town, sampling the delicious outdoor cookery, speaking to as many people as she could, learning current idioms and perfecting her accent still further. She faithfully took her dose of misamine, not fully understanding why she was drawn to it. She wished she could leave it off altogether, since she felt more alert just before taking her dose than afterward. It was usually just before taking the drug that she thought of Carl, remembering the best moments of their all too short time together. She went over and over their first encounter on the desolate streets he liked to frequent. She had thought of those times often, creating for herself a mental snapshot of a Carl that she would almost certainly never see again the same way at the Estate.

Mora had experienced only casual dates before coming to the SOS, and her intimacy with Carl had exceeded her erotic imaginings. As she walked around Guatemala City, she would often receive admiring remarks from passing men, and an occasional backside fondle. She never thought of herself as having any special beauty, but she knew that she made heads turn. Still, in every encounter, she would imagine seeing Carl.

At last she was provided with all necessary papers, and arrangements were made for her to take a commercial airline from Guatemala to Cuba. As she waited in Guatemala City for her flight, she felt no nervousness whatever and certainly no qualms about her mission. The plane arrived, and after a minutely detailed security inspection the passengers were allowed to board. She was on her way to interview Raoul Sandro.

The trip to Havana went as planned. From the start she was fully accepted as the accredited representative of a leftist paper, and she was allowed freedom to roam around all she wanted. She had corresponded in detail with Sandro's staff before coming, and was made to feel she would be welcome at the presidential palace. On the day of her interview, she felt some trepidation, though after going through a final rehearsal of her performance, she felt it would go well.

At Sandro's palace, she gave her name to the security officer. He checked the things she carried carefully, though of course he had no reason to look for the high-tech devices she actually carried.

"Oh, yes, Miss Sanchez," he said. "President Sandro is expecting you. Go right in."

The office was in a retro Cuban style, the sort of furniture and trimmings that would have been current at the time of Castro's successful revolution. It was comfortable and inviting for intimate conversation. Raoul Sandro greeted her warmly. His Spanish had no trace of local accent, as though he had been born in Spain, or at least had studied there.

"Welcome, Miss Sanchez. We are always happy to give interviews to the sympathetic foreign press. So often it is not sympathetic. Perhaps those are the people I should speak to more often, but I am happy you are here, and I hope I can answer your questions."

"I am sure you can, sir. It is a privilege to be here. You are carrying on the work of Fidel Castro, as the world can see. It is an impressive heritage."

"I do not like to think that I am following closely in his footsteps. Fidel was a great man, a great revolutionary. But the revolution is over. I inherited the communist framework, but we have a freely elected representative government here. It is my job to see that our economy flourishes while at the same time our people receive health care, jobs, security in retirement, and the many other things that make people feel secure with their lives."

Mora was drawn to his words. "You have been a model for many leftists in the U.S. Now even people in America who don't often agree with your politics are trying to start some of the same social programs you have had here for a long time. Have you heard of Ed Grendil?" Mora had studied the rudiments of what the Reform Party stood for, and she of course knew that Carl was Ed's son, though he seemed to have no interest in his father's politics.

"I know a little of the new party he has started. It is a hopeful gesture, though the United States has a long way to go."

The interview went on for over two hours. Mora became increasingly agitated, knowing that at some point she must make a move to inject Sandro with neurobots. The time of the interview drew to a close. Sandro rose, and smiled warmly at Mora. She had become almost physically ill. She moved toward him and made a try at launching the neurobots. Her resolve failed, and they fell harmlessly and invisibly to the floor. The removal of Sandro was intended to appear to be from natural causes, so she had no other weapons on her. At this point, though, she had lost all incentive to finish her mission. The emotional encounter had further weakened the effects of the misamine. She became faint and collapsed toward Sandro, grabbing him as she fell to the floor. To a guard at the door, the act looked like an attack. When it was safe for Sandro, he fired a shot at her, hitting her in the middle of her right calf, smashing the bones. She screamed in pain as Sandro moved away. He felt that something potentially dangerous had happened, but he had no idea what it was. The floor was becoming bloody. "Take her to the infirmary," he told the guard.

On the way to the infirmary she was careful to drop the tiny bot discharger on the street, even though it was too small for easy detection. After she received first aid to stanch the bleeding, she was stripped and searched thoroughly. Nothing was found, except a small bottle containing what appeared to be prescription drugs. An officer read through her note pad, and found only a faithful transcription of her interview with Sandro. There seemed to be nothing incriminatory about her, but nevertheless the officer decided to keep her confined in the infirmary for a few days. The doctor told him, "She will need some time to recover even partially. The gunshot shattered the bones. She will be in a cast for a long time, whether or not she gets the specialized surgery she needs for her leg."

Alone in the hospital room, Mora felt she had been lucky to survive, but she was also painfully aware that she had failed her mission. If she returned to the Estate, it would be in shame, and she would expect to receive severe punishment. Her assignment was an important one, and her failure would be a memorable example to others.

Now, late in the day, some food was brought to her. Exhausted, she slept soundly for a few hours. The officer returned in the early morning.

"We identified your medications, except one, this white pill. What is it for?" he asked.

"It is a new drug for depression. I don't remember what my doctor said it was, but it seems to work well for me."

The officer studied her face as she spoke. She was trained to deal with situations like this. He turned away, picked up the pill bottle and returned it to her. "It looks as though everything is in order. You understand that we had to hold you for a while. The incident, while apparently harmless, looked very suspicious at the time. I am sorry that you had to suffer such a painful injury."

"I can understand your being suspicious," she said. "I don't know what happened to me. I don't often faint."

"We will put you on a plane back to Guatemala. You will need more medical attention than we can give you in a short time."

"Thank you."

When she returned to the Tiempo de Fuego office in Guatemala City, she was treated with great respect. Interviews with Sandro had been notoriously difficult to get, and hers was long and revealing. She helped the editor flesh out some of the notes she had taken, and left them with him to do with as he saw fit. She was eager to return to California, in spite of what awaited her there. But the worsening condition of her wound made the trip impossible.

Her broken flesh continued to bleed under the cast, and when a doctor in Guatemala opened it up for cleaning, it became evident that a deep infection had set in. The doctor was concerned about flesh eating bacteria. The wound seemed to improve slightly while open to the air, though the infection was on the point of spreading, perhaps tending even toward blood poisoning. Mora felt too weak and nauseous to attempt the flight back to the U.S., so she resigned herself to spending some time in the hospital in Guatemala City. There was no one to call to come help her. She assumed Carl had finished his mission by now. He would have either returned to the insulated life at the Estate, or at the very worst died while carrying out the mission. She knew nothing about what he had been assigned to do, and she would have been stunned if she were told. Day after day she lay sweating in her bed, plagued by worry about Carl and by fears of losing her leg.

Chapter 18
Home and the Party

The tiny town of Woodville had become a focal point of political activism. Since local services and amenities were almost nonexistent, one of the largest of the derelict industrial buildings had been converted for use as party headquarters, with smaller ones nearby pressed into service as places to sleep and eat for the staff and visitors. The numbers of these were swelling daily, as it seemed that nearly every grass roots dissident and resistance group in the country, even those with only a few members, wanted to have a say in shaping the party platform and to become part of the new activism.

Ed's house was equally busy. He used it to host his most important visitors, to serve them a meal of sorts and to provide a bed. The town so far offered very few amenities beyond a couple of mediocre restaurants. Ed had to begin thinking of moving the party's headquarters to a more urban setting, where better accommodations and services could be arranged. The huge tidal swell of interest in the Reform Party had happened so fast that he hardly had time to review his own positions on all the diverse matters brought before him. In fact, incessant demands and repetitive requests were telling on his resolve to see it through as the principal candidate. Especially after what had already happened to him and his family, he began to wonder if he was as well suited for this role as he had once thought, in spite of the enthusiastic approbation he received daily. He had no training in how to sway people with rhetoric, though he was trying to learn the fundamentals. It was important to him to try to find common ground with those who were not behind him all the way, but who still felt he might be the best option for them. Whether he liked it or not, he was a popular candidate, and had it been just a little more appropriate, he would have been carried on the shoulders of his admirers wherever he appeared. Nevertheless, he thought often of Sikes's demand that he drop out as leader of the party. Maybe Sikes had been right, though for the wrong reasons.

As the campaign hype and accolades intensified, Ed felt more and more detached from the frenzy of party work and fund raising. His life had always been one of thinking alone about a favorite idea, or puttering in his laboratory, usually by himself. The constant demands of the Party were telling on him. He was expected to make public announcements daily, to participate in advertising for the media, give interviews to the press, speak before benefit groups, and gracefully deal with all the other myriad details a candidate has to live through. The activity tired him, and on many an evening he would drop off to sleep while trying to analyze how it all had gotten so out of control in such a short time. He wondered whether it was even important that he be the presidential candidate. Surely, there were dozens of young party members who, he thought, would be more qualified than he. He felt his best role would be that of merely being regarded as the guru who thought the party up, and letting it go at that.

The kidnapping of Max and Anna, the aborted attempt on his life by Carl, the confinement of Anna by Sikes, and the subsequent visit of Lyn to Sikes were all traumatic episodes that took their toll on his resolve and single-mindedness toward the party. He had never before been a model of a devoted family man, but having his family members abused and placed in danger through his having proposed a revolutionary new party made him think deeply about his relationship to them. He was at a crossroads of either choosing to become entirely political or trying to return to a simpler life, a life involving his family. There seemed to be no compromise position.

When Lyn came home with Anna, both of them safely out of Sikes's clutches, Ed felt a joy unlike anything he could remember. He resolved to try to start again with Max, Anna, and Carl and to act more like a father even though they were long past the age of nurturing. He knew he would become closer with Lyn as time went on, but right now he was still dealing with her interest in Sikes. No matter how ephemeral it was, or how necessary, it was still an interest on her part. He did not know how far they had gone together that last time, but since it was his nature to let the past go and not hold grudges, he felt he had to let the events pass. When Lyn and Anna entered the house and saw Ed, they had hugged him tightly, an emotional show of attachment that convinced him that the love of his family was more important than any public accolades he might get.

Anna felt entirely exhausted and bedraggled. She went to her room to try to rest and get herself back to something close to her normal appearance. Lyn took Ed aside. "I have to tell you now. I injected Sikes with the neurobots that Carl gave me. He only has a couple of weeks to live. But I am worried that he may try something before he becomes too mentally destroyed. That would mean the next few days are critical."

Even without knowing the details, the fact that Lyn was the instrument of Sikes's eventual death erased any lingering doubts Ed may have had about her. He wondered briefly whether he should take his family to some sheltered hiding place that Sikes could not locate, at least until they were sure he was dead. Ed could not be sure what methods Sikes would try to use but he was certain there would be a desperate retaliation. He decided they should stay where they were, and simply beef up their guard. The premises were already screened by party members concerned about his security.

While Ed Grendil and his family faced their personal difficulties, there was no lack of success for the Reform Party itself. The polls almost daily reported a greater percentage of the U.S. public behind the fundamental changes it advocated. While almost no one believed that such changes could actually be realized completely, the very idea of their possibility galvanized a hundred million people. The impact of the polls was not lost on incumbent politicians, or the President himself, all of whom were scrambling to propose legislation that would appear to address some of the issues. In his familiar backpedaling mode, the President gave dozens of speeches all over the country, in which he said in effect, "I have always been in favor of these reforms. I have always supported the will of the people. There have been political obstacles, but I guarantee you these will not stand in our way."

After many years of privatizing nearly every aspect of government, of making massive cuts in programs that would benefit the destitute, of almost eliminating subsidized education, of failing the people in times of catastrophic loss, and of keeping the country ground down by endless wars, very few of his former followers felt that his words rang true. Almost nobody believed the President anymore. His speeches were merely a rallying point that drew more people into embracing the Reform Party.

Chapter 19
Sikes

Robert Sikes was angry and befuddled by his recent setbacks. His mind, already clouded by mental deterioration, became obsessed with the feeling that the injection Lyn had just given him was already destroying his brain, though in fact it would take two or three weeks. In desperation, he waited hours for Carl to come with the neurobot antidote. In late afternoon, when it seemed clear that nobody would come, he thought at first that Carl had simply decided not to come. Then his fear grew that perhaps there was no antidote at all. He dreaded calling Thalia to find out, but felt it was his last chance. She answered her private number.

"Thalia, I have been given the neurobots by accident. I was told that an antidote had been developed. I knew the DI was working on something like that. Can I get it now?"

Thalia felt a surge in her stomach. Sikes had at one time been a respected contributor to DI, though she no longer had any personal regard for him. She could not imagine how he became infected, but it didn't matter. If what he had told her was true, Robert Sikes was among the walking dead.

"Robert, there is no antidote. There is no way to communicate with the neurobots."

The phone was silent for a while. "Thank you, Thalia. I should have known."

In spite of her feelings about Sikes, she wished she could give him some slight hope, but there was none. In a week or so he would start showing signs of neural impairment, a speeded up version of what one would expect from brain cancer, although, in the case of the neurobots, the damage would be to several control centers at once, so the symptoms would take wildly oscillating forms. It was an ugly death, involving insanity and pain. But then it would be over, with death preceded by several days of coma. Neurologists called in to diagnose and treat him would find nothing that could respond to surgery or any other treatment. No cancer cells were apparent, so this mainstay diagnosis and treatment would be worthless. All they could do would be to ease the agony with increasing doses of opiates.

"How did it happen, Robert?" she asked.

"It was Ed Grendil's wife. It's a long story, but she got the neurobots from Carl. He did not complete his mission. He's there at home with Ed Grendil."

This put a different light on the event. Carl had failed. There had been plenty of time for Carl to see Ed Grendil, transfer the neurobots, and return to the Estate. He had not come back. The coincidence of this, coupled with the attack on Sikes, made her wonder if some breach in procedures and security had occurred. Still, she was inwardly pleased that Carl was still alive. She had liked both him and Mora from the start, and it was in fact their current assignments that gave her some misgivings about the whole SOS operation.

"We should never have sent Carl on this mission," she said. "I thought it might end differently than we planned, though I didn't expect it to be a complete failure. Carl was trained to use any means to destroy Grendil and himself if need be. Something could have happened to him to cancel the effects of the misamine. I have been getting scattered reports about that happening in other cases. I'll look into it."

Sikes did not share her concerns. He was preoccupied with the dreadful prospect of imminent death. "I would like to see them all dead. I will find a way to get to them. Let me take the percussive devices and the neurobots."

"Sikes," she went on, "You will have to give up on the Ed Grendil mission. I know you have nothing to lose now, and I'm sorry for you, but we can't risk blowing cover on you and especially SOS. Lyn Grendil knows about the bots, which rules out using them. Ed Grendil is a major political candidate now, and killing him in a violent way would create two problems. He would become a martyr and strengthen the party, neither of which the President would like. Further, you might be implicated, and your connections to SOS and DI would be embarrassing to us all. No, I can't see any way that you could reach Ed Grendil with neurobots now and keep it all a secret."

Sikes was in no mood to hear logical reasoning. He pondered the options. Clearly he would have to act on his own. Thalia and the SOS would be of no help.

"I want revenge. I'll do something on my own."

"After all the service you have given us, it's a pity to let it end this way. You will be disavowed completely by the DI, and whatever involvement you have had will be eliminated from the records. Stay here. We will make your last days comfortable."

Sikes was sure the neurobots were already beginning to gnaw at his brain. He was having trouble understanding Thalia. He had to get to Ed's house at once.

"Goodbye, Thalia."

After he left, Thalia notified the DI of his intentions, and they sent agents to try to track him. Suspecting this, he left immediately by a rarely used route and took back roads toward Woodville. His mind was becoming deeply clouded, but his determination to try to destroy Ed Grendil kept it in focus well enough to remember the route. Within two hours he had parked in a secluded part of Woodville, several blocks away from Ed's house. He had brought a small handgun and a knife. He had only to get close enough. It was dark when he arrived. Many party workers had left for the night, though there were still dozens milling around inside the house, finishing various tasks. He could see the guards, sitting quietly by the porch or along the road. He scaled an old rock fence and made his way toward the side of the house, which seemed to be unguarded.

He climbed a trellis and slipped inside an open window. It was one of the bedrooms in which the children had grown up. He opened the door to the central landing, and peered down toward the groups of workers. He did not see Ed but assumed he must be with them. He started down the hallway, and was about to rush down the stairs when a door opened and Lyn stepped out in front of him. They were both surprised, but Lyn acted first. She screamed at him, "You! What are you doing here?" She saw the knife in his hand and lunged at him to try to push him over the railing. He held on to her, and they both fell to the floor.

"You bitch!" Sikes screamed. "You have fucked me up since I first saw you." He plunged the knife into her chest. Within moments after her scream, a guard rushed from one of the upper rooms and tackled Sikes, before he had a chance to pull out his pistol. He tried to slash the guard with his knife, but by that time others had swarmed up the stairs, seizing and pounding him. He closed his eyes and went limp.

When a guard said it was safe, Ed Grendil came from the lower floor and ran up the stairs. He saw Sikes, and the bloody body of Lyn lying inertly on the floor. He fell down beside her and held her head in his hands. The knife had severed a main artery, and it was impossible to stop the blood. He held her even more tightly and began to weep. "I didn't want it to end this way, Lyn. I wanted us to start a whole new life together. I'm sorry. I'm sorry." In a last desperate reflex, she opened her eyes and smiled at him, before becoming unconscious forever.

Once again an overpowering wave of guilt enveloped him. He felt that the whole thing would never have happened had he not tried to reform the world, to start a party so threatening to the power structure. He had no clear idea about the sequence of events that had brought Robert Sikes there that night and resulted in Lyn's death, but he knew that somehow his own actions were involved in them.

He lay on the floor, wet with her blood, shaking with anguish. Carl took him under the arms, lifted him away into a side room and tightly held his wracked body. He said, "Dad, it's over now. They've got Sikes and are turning him over to the police. I think he came to kill you, and mom somehow stopped him. We'll need to wait to piece it together. Let me help you get cleaned up. I'll give you a sedative and you can try to get some sleep. It's a terrible night." He helped Ed into the bathroom, got him washed up and into a bed. There were always sedatives in the medicine cabinets. Carl found them and gave some to Ed with a glass of water. Within minutes, the exhausted Ed Grendil began sleeping, breathing heavily. Carl was almost choking with grief himself, at seeing the dead body of his mother, but somehow he had mustered enough strength to take care of Ed.

Carl left the room and sat on the upper step of the staircase. Anna, who had in horror witnessed most of what had just happened, came to sit beside him. They put their arms around each other and began to cry softly. They stayed this way until they were asked by the police to give their account of what had happened. While they related what they had seen, Max, who had also seen a little of what had happened from the ground floor, simply collapsed into a chair, completely immobilized and unable to comprehend the tragedy.

Chapter 20
The Center Cannot Hold

Sikes, tightly handcuffed and chained, rode to the police station without saying a word. He was asked if he wanted a lawyer and was read his rights. He remained quiet until they were inside the station, seated at a table. "I want to make a public confession," he said. "But before I do it is important that it be given to the media exactly as I give it." The request was unusual, and one of the officers said they would have to wait until a judge cleared it. The procedure took some hours, during which Sikes was kept in a cell under close observation. Finally, a judgment came with the decision that public release would be permitted, as long as it was made clear to Sikes that it would be next to impossible to retract a public confession once it had reached the press. Sikes agreed and asked for a few reporters to be present. When they came, he began to dictate his confession into a small digital recorder as well as to a live court reporter. The media reporters who were present also taped what he said and took notes.

His message was brief. "I, Robert Sikes, confess to entering the house of Ed Grendil with the intention of killing him and others of his family if possible. I acted on orders received from the President to kill Ed Grendil, though killing the others was my idea. Grendil's wife, Lyn, betrayed me a week ago when she came to my house and injected me with neurobots, a development by the Division of Intelligence under my own direction. I am happy that I killed Lyn Grendil. I did not have a chance to kill Ed Grendil's son Carl, but I would have if I could. He also betrayed me by failing in the mission I had given him to remove Ed Grendil using neurobots, on orders from the President. What I am saying is the complete truth. I have no reason to lie now. I will be dead within two weeks."

Sikes was taken away to a cell to await arraignment. The police officers were thrown completely off guard when they heard his confession. The Chief immediately recognized its sensitive content and the risk to national security were it made public. He felt that releasing it in its raw state was simply impossible, even though permission for release had been cleared by a judge. Sikes's lawyer agreed that the contents of the confession would need additional clearance, in the interest of national security. The reporters present, however, had an entirely different idea, and that was to get it into the media stream as quickly as possible. It was the kind of news story that would galvanize the entire country, and they felt it was entirely legitimate to release it, since it had the approval of a prior judgment. The Chief first attempted to threaten the reporters with arrest and confinement if they did not give up their recordings and notes, though he knew that such an extralegal action would almost certainly wreck his career. He reverted to emotionally pleading with the press to delay the story, and eventually a standoff was reached when the risky consequences of releasing the story began to be realized by the reporters themselves. After more discussion with the Chief they agreed to hold up submitting the story, at least for a short time while the DI could examine the confession and speak further to Sikes. They would wait until they heard from the DI, within two days at a maximum.

The DI agent put in charge of the confession information was none other than Bob Smith, the pseudonymous agent who had helped arrange for Carl to be inducted into the SOS, something that Ed Grendil had come to regret bitterly. Smith realized that the Sikes confession could not be kept secret for long. The few days the reporters had agreed to was the best the DI could hope for. They would have to use the time in devising spins to downplay the confession as much as possible. Since Sikes's involvement with the SOS was directly mentioned, Smith made contact with Thalia M'Gos to advise her of the impending storm. He could not be certain, but he hinted to her that eventual disbanding of the SOS would be inevitable and that it might be wise for her to begin preparing now for its demise. This would mean aborting missions where possible and demobilizing the Soldiers. Knowledge of the missions themselves must be destroyed, lest international repercussions from the many target removals create an untenable political climate for the U.S.

Thalia had already deduced that the SOS was on its way toward public exposure, which would mean its end. Knowledge of the Sikes confession merely confirmed her conclusions. In the meantime, however, she had to continue acting as director, trying to provide support for returning Soldiers, whether they had successfully finished their missions or not. Mora Sanchez was one such Soldier, and she remembered that Mora and Carl had become intimate with each other. She had inwardly hoped that somehow they would get together again, though the chance now seemed impossibly remote. As she pondered the interconnections among the Grendil family, the SOS, and Sikes, she was awed by how a small chain of events could bring down so much. She refused to dwell on her own fate after the end of the SOS, a kind of denial that had worked for her in other difficult times.

Although Sikes's murder of Lyn had devastated Carl, he could not put thoughts of Mora from his mind, nor his great concern about what may have happened to her on her mission. Now that he had become free of his narcotic compulsion to obey as a member of the SOS, he was sorry he couldn't have given her the antidote to the addictive SOS pills, just the way his father had given it to him. Regardless of what was happening at his father's house, the well being of Mora became the most important thing in his life. There was a slim chance that Thalia, as SOS director, would know where she was, and what had happened to her, but it was indeed slim, especially since he had failed his mission. One of the DI rules was not to make inquiries about an SOS mission, for security reasons. Instead, the policy was to wait until the Soldier returned home, successful or not.

He did have one hope. The F-chip implants they had all received when they entered the SOS were still in place. The reason for this chip at all was to enable communication in dire situations. Usually this meant Soldiers transmitting something out to signify success or failure of a mission shortly before sacrificing themselves. By the nature of the chip design, however, it was possible to communicate to the Soldier. Carl had to find out from Thalia whether he could make such a call, but given his present status he knew that this may be difficult. His own communication system was designed to operate only between him and the Estate.

Returning to the Estate was risky. He could not guess how much Thalia knew of his recent activities, though Sikes must have told her what had happened with the aborted action against Ed Grendil and of Lyn's infecting him with neurobots. She still may not know of Sikes's last ditch suicide attempt to remove Ed himself, an effort that also had failed. Carl, as far as he knew at the moment, ran the risk of being seized, or even shot on the spot as a renegade. He could not predict the vengefulness of the SOS administrators, or even of Thalia, whom he had met many times in friendly settings. Still, he had to take the chance.

He activated his palm chip and waited for a connection. He had never used this method before, so he was surprised when it actually worked. A voice asked him to identify himself with a code number. Carl gave it and asked if he could speak to Thalia directly. He was told that she was not feeling well, but that a connection might be possible. After a few more minutes, he heard her voice, sounding faint and a bit wobbly, but distinct.

"Thalia, this is Carl. I'd like to talk to you. I failed in my mission."

"Yes, I know you did. We will speak of that. Come to my office."

Her stern tone made him apprehensive. He wondered if he could trust her. "I am worried that if I come there I will be punished, maybe put to death."

"No, that will not happen now. I give you my word on that." She went on to give him driving directions. He thought it would take no more than two hours.

When he pulled up to the locked entrance gate, he was still apprehensive. Words with a robotic attendant were relayed to Thalia, and she opened the gate. He drove to a place near her office. The campus seemed nearly deserted, different from when he was last there. He knocked lightly on Thalia's door and went in. She sat low in her chair, looking tired and pale.

"Much has happened here since you left, Carl. It looks as though we will be disbanding completely before long." The full impact of Sikes's confession had not yet reached the press, but word that it soon would had reached her from the DI.

Carl was indeed surprised at this news. When he first joined, he had felt the aims and methods of the SOS were ideally suited for the state of public opinion at the time. The majority in the U.S. had turned against the endless wars that had taken hundreds of thousands of traditional Soldiers, and countless numbers of mostly innocent civilians. The SOS with its selective removal of troublemakers around the world seemed a perfect solution.

"Can you talk about what has happened?" he asked. Carl sensed that she was not only willing to ignore his status as a failed Soldier, but that she needed someone, a familiar face, to talk to.

"There were many problems," she said. "There is much concern about the cruelty of using the neurobot method that Sikes had developed. Also, we have always depended on a drug called misamine to help maintain a high performance level among our Soldiers, to give them a joyous feeling about being involved in such a useful common effort. It started to have problems, to the point that sometimes our Soldiers on a mission would find themselves without its emotional support. I think you probably had an experience like that."

"I withdrew from it myself," Carl said. "Perhaps it was the emotion of my mission, or my fixation on some earlier experiences when I was alone, but whatever it was, I wanted to stop the drug. I hadn't realized there was an addictive part to it, but luckily for me my father had the right counteragent."

Thalia went on, "The final blow was the confession made by Robert Sikes. It will be made public very soon, and the secrecy of our mission will be highly compromised. We still have some soldiers out on duty, but the SOS is coming to an end. The political situation in Washington is in chaos. You cannot imagine what impact the sudden rise of the Reform Party has made. That, coupled with the Sikes confession, has imperiled the entire program. It is too late, of course, but the President and the representatives are trying to act as though they wanted to do the same things as the RP all along. The chief idea that affects the SOS directly is the one from the

Reform Party that says the U.S. hardly needs a military force at all, other than something like the National Guard, and that we should cease and desist altogether from trying to impose our particular form of government on the rest of the world."

"I heard about that from my father and mother before she was killed. I hadn't known much about the Reform Party until I went home recently. I've never been much interested in politics, but I suppose I will now that my dad has become so identified with it."

"I probably would, too, if I were you. Perhaps I will after I'm out of a job, if I can get through that part successfully. But you didn't come here to talk about politics," she said.

"No, I came to see whether I can get in touch with Mora."

"We haven't heard from her. It's our usual policy not to try to contact Soldiers on a mission, for reasons of security and safety. She has not attempted to reach us, as far as I know. It has been a long time."

"I'm worried about her. We had become close. Can you try to reach her? It would mean a lot to me." Carl was grasping at any possibility, though he doubted that Thalia would be much help.

To his surprise, she said, "Usually, this would be an impossible request. But I will see what we can do." She called her communications officer and asked for his help. He said it could be done, provided Mora's equipment was still functioning. He patched an audio line to Thalia's desk and signaled Mora. Nothing came through. After nearly an hour of trying, she told him to go back to his old rooms and wait. The communications officer would call him if he could reach her.

Carl waited in his rooms the rest of the day. He became convinced it was a hopeless idea. He called Thalia and told her he was leaving the Estate to go home. She said they would continue to try, though it did not look promising. Then, to everyone's surprise, the line from Mora opened up, and she was put through to Carl. She had a hard time speaking and her voice was very weak, but she spoke directly to Carl.

"Oh, Carl. I never expected to hear from you. I am not doing too well here. My leg seems to be getting worse. I don't know whether it will all work out or not. I failed in my mission." She was uncharacteristically sniffling a little.

"Yes, I know about that. I'll come to take you back. Maybe getting treatment here will help. I have been talking to Thalia. It should be safe for you to come back, even if the mission didn't go well. Things have changed here. The SOS will be folding up altogether soon. People are dropping out all the time."

Mora gave him the name of the hospital she was in and said she would promise to hang on until he got there. Carl called Ed Grendil to let him know of these new developments, and asked him to help get plane tickets. Carl had a passport, issued by the SOS, and no visa was needed. He left immediately for Guatemala City. He had not eaten in a day, and no food was available on the plane. His cheap seat, surrounded by families with noisy children, put him in a gloomy and restive mood that grew worse the more he thought of Mora's plight.

Chapter 21
Anna and the Party

As expected, the Sikes confession was a bombshell. Other than the sketchy mention he had made of neurobots, there was no account available of the way a person dies when infected with them, so the press eagerly looked forward to putting out daily progress reports on Sikes's condition to a huge and expectant audience. Denials and explanations about the confession came quickly and in volume from the White House. The primary position of the administration was that this meaningless babble came from a man who had already become insane from an accidental infection by one of his inventions. Sikes's involvement with secret weapons of this kind was well documented, and the confession represented just the ravings of a mind going under.

At first the DI had wanted to keep the details of the way Sikes died a secret, but orders from the top indicated that it was to be a public viewing. A week after his confession was made public, Sikes was experiencing the full force of the neurobots tearing at his brain tissue. His angry outbursts died away, replaced by bits of description of his past, reminiscent of the dying computer Hal in the movie. But when other nerve centers were affected, he began moaning and then screaming. It became clear that increasing dosages of morphine were necessary. Then nothing more was needed. Sikes stared straight ahead for a few hours then died when neural control over his vital functions was disrupted.

Public viewing of Sikes before and during his death throes was a calculated antidote to any belief in the veracity of Sikes's confession. Clearly, it seemed to be merely the raving of a madman. It had the effect of keeping the country temporarily calm, but overall the credibility of the administration was severely shaken. The affair turned many more people toward support of the Reform Party, already experiencing unprecedented popularity. To its platform was added rejection of nearly all of the secretive information mining activities that were enabled under the guise of helping the U.S. battle its covert enemies. The clincher, in the popular mind, was the Reform Party's formal adoption of a policy of not initiating physical interference with the governments of other countries.

After the traumatic events of the recent past, Ed Grendil began trying to recover something of a normal life. Having his wife Lyn die while trying to prevent a deranged former associate from killing him was hardly something to put aside. At least the intense party activities furnished an outlet that could take up all his time, if he so desired. In an oblique way, he enjoyed the attention given to him and the power of being the leader, but gradually he came to realize that there were others who might take on the mantle of party leader more effectively than he. And to him it was important that the party ideals prevail, not those of whoever happened to be a candidate.

Anna, too, had difficulties in regaining her life after the death of Lyn, who had, after all, been the one who saved her from Sikes, although Anna came to realize that her mother was also to blame for much of Sikes's insane vindictiveness toward the whole family. She at first wanted to have nothing to do with the party activities, and seriously considered going to the eastern part of the country to continue her volunteer work. The turning point in her life was a routine end-of-the-week party given at Ed's house for the inner core party workers. She attended, not because of any special enjoyment of such events, but to please Ed, who liked to be seen with his children as often as possible. A few reporters were present, casually asking off-the-cuff questions. One of them approached her.

"Miss Grendil, my name is Eric Claver. May I ask you a couple of questions?"

"Yes, of course. Nothing political, I hope. I'm only slightly connected to the party."

"More than slightly, I think. Let me start with this question. How well did you know Robert Sikes?"

Anna answered quickly, "He was a fixture around the house when I was a kid. After I left home, I hardly thought of him."

"Why did you leave home?"

"Why do any kids leave home? I was a teenager, restless, doing things my parents either didn't approve of, or that they didn't understand, like music."

"What made you come back?"

"I don't know exactly how to answer that. I sensed that something wasn't quite right between my parents. And Carl had decided to go off with some kooky military group called the SOS."

The reporter continued, "Did you know anything about that group?"

"Almost nothing. I had heard from Dad that it could be a good experience for Carl, to give his life some structure, and so forth. All the things parents like to see their kids doing. Hey, to cut short some of your questions, let me say that I was very worried about Carl. He seemed mixed up in something that was quite unlike the way I knew him. I wanted to come back and help. That's why I got in touch with Sikes. That's all I want to say right now."

The reporter would like to have gone on, but folded his notebook, thanked Anna, and started to walk away.

She called to him. "Say, Eric Claver, let's go over to the bar and have a drink."

Claver was surprised and pleased. Anna was the kind of person he liked, forthright, honest. But also he found her highly appealing as a woman. She had much of the same animal-like activity level of her father, with a slightly asymmetric angelic face that might be called spiritual, were either she or Eric inclined that way. She had strength and detachment unlike anyone he had met.   In other circumstances, he would have approached her himself. As a reporter, it did not seem appropriate, since it may seem he was compromising his objectivity. But she had asked him.

"I'm up for that," he said.

The Angelou Café had installed a proper bar to accommodate the new people in town. It was plain but quiet and private enough for Anna and Eric. They sat for a long time, not going any deeper into her personal motivations, just exchanging phatic pleasantries about what they liked to do, the kinds of people that bored them or excited them, and so on. They touched hands, but eventually they both began to feel exhausted and parted from each other with a simple goodbye.

Their unassuming beginning grew into an off-and-on romantic involvement, one that flared whenever they saw each other in some casual setting but which did not at first seem to be leading anywhere. They sometimes drove to the city to see a movie but came back soon after it was over and continued to exchange only a polite kiss on parting. Then one night, Anna asked Eric to her room. They put on some music, a contemporary piece Carl had given her, and during a soft adagio part they undressed and got into bed, without a word. Next morning, without expressing it to each other, they both felt that their lives had changed. Eric was convinced he had found the love of his life. Anna may have felt a little of that, but she had an overpowering sense that she was entering a relationship that frightened her because she feared its eventual constrictions. For now she wanted no part of it.

Eric continued reporting the party's activities, as well as he could, but he also began spending more and more time helping with party work. His journalistic training was valuable in producing press releases and in advising field workers about developing skills in public relations. The popularity of the party and its aims continued to grow, and Eric wanted to have a part in that growth. He encouraged Anna toward more involvement herself, both with the party and with him, though her reticence toward any permanent relationship, especially marriage, seemed as unbending as ever. He resolved to stay with the party regardless of how their affairs turned out and create a new career for himself.

Chapter 22
Mora returns

When Carl arrived in Guatemala City in midafternoon, a tropical storm had blown in from the west, bringing hot rains and high winds. Before going to the hospital, he stopped briefly under the covered seating of an open air restaurant for something to eat, since the plane had offered nothing. The waiter apologized for the sparse menu, but it was adequate and Carl settled on a tamale-like dish with a beer. It was the first alcohol he'd tasted in a year. He felt a little guilty at not rushing immediately to Mora's side, but knew he would need some energy when he did find her. The hospital was not far from the restaurant. As he walked, he couldn't help but notice the sunlight filtering through the tropical trees on the tiled sidewalk. He thought of those simpler times before all the recent terrible events, and felt that somehow, with Mora safe at home with him, it would be like that again. He wasn't sure that she would like to lead as reclusive a life as he did, but then he looked forward to adapting to her way of living as well.

He saw the hospital ahead, slightly rundown but obviously in heavy use. He entered the hospital lobby and asked a nurse behind the desk for Mora Sanchez. She shrugged slightly and said something in Spanish that he didn't understand. He mustered his limited knowledge of the language and asked, "Cual sala?" She looked oddly at him, then pointed toward a hallway, saying in English, "Number 24." She shrugged again, with a shake of her head. He opened the door quietly. The bed was empty. He rushed to it and ripped away the sheet. A bloody spot remained where her leg must have lain. She was gone.

He rushed back to the nurse. "Where is she?" he cried, "How could she have left?"

The nurse looked startled. She actually spoke English fairly well. "A man came with papers and took her away. He said he was from the American military. He looked like an official. She was not a Guatemalan, so it seemed all right to release her."

"When did they leave?"

"Early this morning. There is a plane to California then."

Carl went back to Mora's room and sat for a while on the bed. He touched the spot of blood. Had he only acted sooner, he thought, he may have come to the hospital before the agent. He felt a wave of despair, and a sense that he would never see her again. From what he had gleaned from Thalia, the SOS was being dismantled, and Soldiers on assignments were being brought back by DI agents, all under the strictest secrecy. Undoubtedly, the orders from Washington were to make it appear that the SOS never existed. The fact that Mora had failed in her mission might make her continued existence even riskier. He had to find her somehow.

During the return flight next morning, he tried to sketch a plan, but nothing seemed to gel. The DI agent had probably taken her to a central lockup somewhere, and he would have no further communication with her. When he landed, he called Thalia. She was almost on her way out. "They will be closing the gates for good, Carl. A lot of the Soldiers have been taken away into what they call protective custody. I don't know where they will take Mora. I wish I could help you. I really do."

"Thanks, Thalia. You've done all you can. I hope things work out for you. Good luck."

Thalia stared after him, pondering her own situation. She thought she would need more than luck to get safely away from the sinking SOS. She was too prominent an administrator to be forgotten about. Depending on the thoroughness and intensity of the housecleaning operation, she may be let off with another lesser position somewhere, or none at all, or she may simply disappear. She thought of trying to escape back to Africa, but there was nothing at all for her there. She would be regarded suspiciously as a foreigner. No, she would have to take her chances in the U.S. She had done all she could to help Carl, and wished him well, though she knew not to expect anything from him. After they parted, he made no further efforts to keep in touch with her. He simply assumed later that she had safely survived, though how he did not know.

Carl returned to Woodville with no clear ideas about how to even begin to try to find Mora. The planning sessions for the Reform Party were still in full swing, though many were wondering whether they could withstand the barrage of new proposals coming from Washington. Many of them sounded as though they were copied from the RP plank. Carl greeted the people he knew, then went to his room. He could not stay in that pressured environment for long. His thoughts alternated between happy remembrances of his and Mora's times together and the deepest of black despair at perhaps losing her for good.

His therapy had always been to go to the Zone for his personal variety of meditation, contemplation of the old familiar forms of light and shadow. He never thought he would be spending his days doing this again, but it seemed the only way he could cope with the stress of recent events. All he could do was wait, but wait for what? Would they send out an announcement of her death? Perhaps he would hear only from a newspaper clipping saying that she had died in some kind of duty.

During the rainy season, tiny weeds sprang up from even the smallest cracks in the streets and sidewalks. He got some pleasure from contemplating how life hangs on and survives even in the most hostile places. The weeds could never mature to large plants, but they survived nevertheless, probably even flowering and putting out seeds. As the season became more dry, the weeds began to die. He brought a little water each day, but even with that help the weeds eventually died when they reached their natural span.

He returned to taking photographs of the geometries in the Zone, but it was only in a half hearted way. He usually didn't even look at the results, but it kept him focused on something outside of himself and his despair. He often sat on the stone block where he and Mora had first met. While he was there one day, he had a momentary hallucination of seeing Mora coming down the street toward him. He had relived his first glimpse of her many times, and at first he thought he was seeing merely another illusion from his memory. The figure he saw, definitely a woman, seemed to be moving painfully, and certainly not dancing with youthful exuberance the way Mora had when they first met. Nevertheless, she looked more and more like Mora to him. He briefly wondered if he was going mad. The figure became larger and he could see her face.

He could not believe his eyes. It was indeed Mora, hobbling slowly toward him on crutches. He rushed to meet her. She was exhausted from her exertion but plainly ecstatic at seeing Carl. He threw his arms around her, lifted her up with the crutches clattering to the street. "Oh, Mora," he said, "I never thought I'd see you again." She said the same. It seemed such a cliché to both of them, but they loved it. He took her to a bench on the side of the street where they sat trying to catch up with what had happened. They could hardly talk with the joy of being together again.

She told him of her injury and how the local doctors had wanted to remove her leg, but that she had refused in hopes that somehow she would be taken back where it would be saved. After Carl called her while she was in the hospital, she became convinced that he would come to her and bring her to the U.S. where she could be treated. Instead, a DI agent came to her room, as a visitor. He gave her a large dose of misamine, and told her he would bring her back home for treatment and release. Her resolve weakened, and she went willingly with the agent, ending up back in California at a squalid detention center. She realized that he had been lying all along. There would be no treatment, or release. During her confinement the condition of her leg worsened, and she began to think she would soon die in isolation.

She sat for hours by the small window, marking the passage of time as a succession of gray overcast days or bright sunny ones. Then, for no reason that she could guess, or was ever told, a guard came to her room to tell her to get ready to leave. He would offer no explanation, other than that the SOS was no longer functioning. She asked to be driven somewhere because of her difficulty in walking. She did not want to go directly to the Grendil house on her own, since it was hardly neutral territory, or so she thought. She convinced the guard to take her to the old industrial area, the Zone, where she had first met Carl. It was isolated enough to be neutral. He left her at the place where she had first walked up to Carl. She thought that if he was not there, she could somehow manage to walk on to the house, which was not far away, and take her chances.

Mora and Carl could not know it at the time, but Thalia had been able to influence the DI agents to let Mora go. It was almost her last act before leaving the sinking SOS ship, which was definitely in its last stages. She liked Carl, and believed that this one last act would make no difference in her future. She spoke directly to the agent in charge of bringing Mora back, and was able to convince him that in view of the loss of the SOS, it would make no difference one way or the other in the fate of the former members.

Carl and Mora slowly made their way back to the house. When she became weak from the exertion, he carried her the rest of the way. He was distressed at how light she felt, and it was apparent from the gauntness of her face that her physical condition needed urgent attention. Ed Grendil greeted them at the door, surprised that Carl had not asked him for help but overjoyed that at least this part of their lives seemed to be working out. Carl had told him everything about Mora, and Ed already felt as though she was part of the family. A few of the party workers took charge of her, providing a bath and a little cosmetic work. In the meantime, others made arrangements for her to get immediate surgical attention for her leg. As it turned out, she needed several operations, and with the necessary time between them, the whole procedure was quite drawn out. Carl took complete charge of her care, finding food she liked, helping with physical therapy, but most of all just being there with companionship and talk. The days they had both spent with the SOS seemed to fade into a blur of indistinct memories. They had been in a kind of drugged fog at that time, but nevertheless they remembered in detail their last meeting before going separately to their missions. They resolved to keep the feeling they had then alive.

Chapter 23
Max

Max had been emotionally dependent on Anna for his whole life, a situation that she was not happy about though she could see no alternatives. He had joined her when she moved east some years before, and they lived there together as brother and sister until their return to California and their misguided attempt to influence Ed Grendil to drop out as Reform Party leader. Though they lacked the genetic duplication of identical twins, even fraternally they seemed uncannily close to each other, anticipating thoughts and communicating silently in ways that they used to jokingly call ESP. When Anna returned to the Grendil house after her release by Sikes, she and Max spent much less time together and never resumed the closeness of living in the same rooms together, even though his emotional dependence on her was vastly greater after the murder of his mother.

The depth of his dependence on Anna became apparent the more she sought to define her own life. When they were together, she had organized their meals, their social life, and their entertainment. She had asked him to carry out some duties, but she had planned it all. When they separated, Max was lost. He had no interest in helping Ed in party activities, nor did he develop any activities that he enjoyed on his own. He had no friends other than Anna, so he became a hermit within the house. He rarely left his room, often sitting for hours looking out onto the green landscape with its rolling tree-covered hills with occasional houses. He was prescribed a succession of medications for depression, none of which seemed to do more than act as a mild palliative. He came to look more toward Carl for close bonding rather than to Anna, though both of whom had become more and more involved with others. If those relationships became permanent, Max would be cut adrift.

He loved silly little jokes, especially those involving animals, and very often had one to relate to the family, telling it in a slightly hesitant way but with a little smile that betrayed his pleasure. Anna, Carl, and Ed usually listened patiently, but often without appreciation. Max tried to throw his energy into painting, but he realized after a time that he did not have the dedication, the single mindedness, that would take him to higher levels. He would always be just the novice. And as for his finding a partner like his siblings, he had never had any companionship, male or female, except the asexual closeness of his sister Anna, and his adored mother Lyn.

His thoughts went more and more often to Lyn. He had no religious background whatever and no belief in any kind of existence after death. If he thought about it much at all, he felt that the idea of meeting her in another life was merely a fictional fantasy mirroring the thoughts of those who did believe. But something oddly comforting drew him to the idea that she may have some sort of life after death, and that he may one day see her again. As Anna and Carl became more involved with their lovers, he substituted their friendship with more frequent visits to Lyn's grave. There, in the dark glades of the small Woodville cemetery, he seemed to find a genuine peace. Sometimes he would splay his body over the slight grassy mound of her grave, softly murmuring his hopes that he would at some time join her.

Max used to enjoy telling a macabre story he had heard of a Soldier being given an award. The general tied the medal so tightly around the Soldier's neck that he strangled to death. After some experimenting, Max devised a similar way to choke himself to death with a cord after he had handcuffed his hands behind his back.

No one in the family had any inkling beforehand that Max would ever consider taking his own life. Afterward, they all realized that he had given warning signs that they might have recognized had they not been preoccupied with their own thoughts and problems. Whatever the intention of the one who dies, a suicide causes intense personal reevaluation by the survivors. They met to speak of such things privately after Max's funeral ceremony, after they had received the metallic urn containing Max's ashes. Their words were almost incoherent as each tried to speak of his or her own part in

Max's life and death. Ed Grendil, who had lost both his wife and now his son, seemed to take it hardest, blaming himself for the lack of involvement in his family during the important years when they were all at home together. Anna, remembering the years when she and Max had shared their lives so closely, felt that she should have continued at least a pretense of that relationship, though realistically she knew it could not happen if she wanted to find a life for herself, especially since Eric had come into her life. Carl, who had not been especially close to Max since they were children together, looked upon his own solitary life as a failure to reach out to his brother. The time they all stood together around the urn seemed endless, but in fact was only a few minutes. When they all parted, they realized that the intention of their gathering was expiation, and that had not happened. They tried in vain to see in the polished surface of the urn some kind of image of the Max they remembered, a gentle, shy, and smiling young man who always seemed in the background. Perhaps there was never a strong and realistic image at all, but their imaginary one would stay them for all their lives.

Chapter 24

The Party's Over

The impact of Max's death, so soon after Lyn's, deepened the gloomy pall over the Grendil house. Normally upbeat party workers who were struggling to shape future policy statements found it difficult to come up with cheerful rhetoric. Ed Grendil was profoundly saddened by Max's death. They had not been close, though Max would have liked it. Ed's way of living, of pushing himself to the limit, first in his technical work and now in politics, left no time for interacting with someone like Max, whose modest interests and seeming lack of ambition lay at an opposite pole. Ed took upon himself blame for the suicide, just as he had made himself into the cause of Lyn's death, and found himself moving perilously close to the edge of serious depression. In his inevitable reevaluation of his life, he began to question his function and usefulness as leader of the new party. Important as many had come to think of his role as the founding party mentor, it was starting to seem to him that had he taken a different direction, perhaps the two people now dead may have been saved. But even aside from such self-recrimination, he felt himself becoming distracted, experiencing more and more difficulty staying abreast of changes taking place daily in the country, much less feeling able to assimilate the myriad new details he would be expected to know as a leading candidate, even if he had no chance of winning. Perhaps the stress he had placed himself under was beginning to make the physical effects of his age more apparent. He began to hint to his staff, almost joking about it at first, that he may like to turn the prime candidacy over to someone else. He explained that he would back that person fully, campaigning as much as he could, but that he had to have some time to himself to recover from his own recent personal losses. There were protestations from his party supporters, but in the background some felt that Ed's early and candid protestations of inadequacy and indifference could only lead to better planning, perhaps in helping put Ed back on track or as last resort finding a new candidate. Ed was carrying too much extraneous baggage to remain powerful in a vicious campaign in his present state. The opposition would murder him, this time figuratively, but no less effectively.

None of Ed's doubts was known except to a few intimates. Most people, including his political opponents in Washington, still viewed him as a powerful advocate of radical reform, and he had to admit to himself that the thought of upsetting entrenched political dogma still gave him a shiver of excitement. Without actually knowing any details, he suspected that the two parties in Washington were going through what was often called an agonizing reappraisal. The political leaders from both parties, the ones who were responsible for the country's problems in the first place, were frantically backpedaling to try to make themselves look innocent. There was a rare flurry of bipartisan legislation, a surprising amount apparently borrowed from the campaign statements of the Reform Party. Plans were being drawn up to propose deprivatizing those programs that impacted the entire public, including health care, catastrophe insurance, sustainable national energy, solid planks that Ed Grendil had built into the platform of the Reform Party. Of course, promises and plans come cheap. Implementation was a thing of the future, and the President still seemed strongly opposed to any such changes.

There were no external signs that the Reform Party was weakening in any way. On the contrary its strength grew explosively. The polls indicated that over half the voters supported it and would so vote if the election were immediate. Nevertheless, the divisive strategy of the administration was working. Demonstrations had become calmer and less frequent. People were no less suspicious and contemptuous of the President, but they began to listen to him more calmly as he paid lip service toward embracing some reform, little knowing that his own views were implacably against it.

Frightened but energized by the legislative moves toward enacting some of the Reform Party proposals, the President was advised to ask Ed Grendil to the White House to participate in a kind of peace conference. The plan was to offer a number of "key" positions to the leaders of the RP, especially Ed Grendil himself. As history shows, nothing dilutes the zeal of reform more than bureaucratic sluggishness. By the time it came to presidential veto of the legislative proposals, the firebrands of the RP would be snugly behind their desks, deluding themselves that their beloved reforms were actually in process.

Although none of this Machiavellian scheming was made public, many in the RP were vigorously opposed to Ed's visiting with the President at all. Their gut feeling, correct enough, was that it represented simply another maneuver by the administration to undermine the party. But Ed decided to go. Naive as he was in the wiles of serious politics, he felt that some rapprochement might smooth the way toward implementing the reforms. Besides, his refusal and absence might become viewed as a public failure on his part. In his view, it did not matter how the reforms happened, it mattered only that they were. He felt strongly that the RP reforms required a much larger power base than the Reform Party itself could muster in one election, or maybe ever. He reflected on the campaigning of Eugene Debs, who was repeatedly trounced but had some of his ideas incorporated into the New Deal.

The President greeted him warmly. "Hello, Mr. Grendil. I'm sorry we haven't met before, but better late than never, eh?" He had a hollow kind of chuckle that never seemed sincere, but Ed ignored it. He had heard it many times during broadcasts.

"Well, it has to have something to do with the success of the Reform Party, doesn't it. You wouldn't have even heard of me without it."

"That's right. Sometimes it takes something like an earthquake to wake us up. We've learned a lot about how the people feel from your party efforts. We need to make some changes." He chuckled again.

Ed did not smile. "I've heard there's some legislation being talked about that would duplicate some of the Reform Party platform. I suppose one would be justified in being a little skeptical until there were some results."

"You bet. You should be. Many a cup, you know."

"Yes, sir."

The confession made by Robert Sikes had become public knowledge, played frequently on the various media outlets, and the administration's explanations and denials were given equally generous coverage. The public viewing of the mental state of Sikes was convincing evidence that whatever he had done or said, it was the output of a raving madman. It became important to the administration to distance itself from this lunatic.

"That Sikes thing was a mess. I don't know how he ever came up with the idea that getting rid of you would solve our problems. That so-called 'confession.' I'm glad it's been found out to be just the babbling of a nut case."

Lyn had never told Ed that Sikes had been commissioned by the President to try to kill him. Ed's having known Sikes through many turbulent years made it easy to believe that his actions were the result of a seriously deteriorated mind, just as the president was saying.

"That's all behind us now. Sikes is dead."

"Yes. He let the whole country down by acting like such an idiot. But I wanted to speak more of your future. The Reform Party. How is it going?"

Ed felt the President was leading up to something, but he gave a straight answer. "The percentage figures speak for themselves, don't they? It's an amazing runaway thing. I don't think anyone realized how unhappy the voting public was."

"But what about your own part in it?"

Ed was not sure how to answer. All the doubts he had since Lyn's death, and now Max's suicide, flooded back. "I must confess I have had some doubts as to whether I want to continue to run. It's one thing to run, another to win and have the country's problems dumped in your lap."

"That's right. Good."

"The object of the party was to get some major changes in the country's directions. Another candidate may be better at getting things done than I. I don't know. Besides, if the present administration does its part, then maybe some of what the Reform Party advocates may be accomplished more quickly than if we had to start from scratch."

"Just what I want to talk to you about. I've been thinking about the new legislation that's coming down the wire. You've got a bunch of guys that know all about this stuff. We could fit them in to new positions in the departments, where they could see to implementing things without the country having to jump through its asshole to get there. No need to overthrow the whole system. What do you think?"

Ed paused for a minute or so. He wanted to go cautiously. "You said 'guys.' There are a lot of women in the Reform Party, too."

"Oh, hell, I know that," the President responded. "There's room for everybody in this administration."

"What sort of position would I have?"

"You can chart your own course. I'd think you would want some control over the others. We could come up with some kind of cabinet level slot if we need to."

Ed leaned back in his chair, hands at the back of his head, eyes closed. After a few minutes, the President said, "I know it's a big decision. Why don't you go outside for a while and think about it. I've still got a country to run here, you know." He ended with a characteristic mirthless laugh.

Ed's decision was made by that little laugh. He got up, went to the outer room and strolled along slowly, looking at the paintings, while being closely watched by an array of guards. He was in no hurry, and made no move to resume his chat with the President. Finally, the door to the Oval Office burst open, with another cheery, "Come back in."

"Well, what do you think of the idea now? We could really make some progress together with this one."

"Mr. President, I've never called anyone a flat-out liar before, especially the president of my country, but I think you've lied to me. I don't believe for a minute that you will stand aside while the kind of reforms our party has been proposing could be enacted. You remember the old song 'Take This Job and Shove It?' Well, I'll be going back to my supporters and associates with this message, 'I told the President to take his proposal and shove it.'"

The President's face reddened as he stood up and said, "I'm sorry that Sikes bastard fucked up." He pressed a button and an agent immediately entered.

"Escort this son of a bitch out of here. We have no more to say to each other." These were indeed the last words he said to Ed.

Chapter 25
Connecting the Dots

When Ed left the President's office he walked toward the Mall. The air was crisp with the onset of fall and acted on him as a restorative. As he walked slowly back toward his hotel, he began a mental game of placing the recent events of his life into scenes of a play in which he had the leading role Or sometimes he would merely see them as vividly colored images in the backdrop. Either way it seemed theatrical enough that he could detach himself and find comfort from the painful reality of his memories. Even though his tendency to blame himself for what had happened within his family had hardly changed, he felt that he was on the verge of developing an ability to look at these dreadful events in a more detached way. He knew that somehow he would again muster enough strength to challenge this President and his administration.

When he returned to Woodville, his first hours were spent with party colleagues, briefing them on the conversation he'd had with the President, and suggesting some strategy about using the President's arrogant attitudes for the benefit of the Reform Party. Before his trip to Washington, his associates were already quietly evaluating the consequences of his resigning, and that they may have to find another candidate. They dreaded this crises, and although Ed did not immediately disabuse them of his earlier hints about resigning, from his very silence on the matter and his enthusiastic way of making strategy suggestions his colleagues began to take heart that he would "stay the course," as an earlier president often said, and regain his old enthusiasm. He privately knew he would be able to continue even stronger than before, but he was still too emotionally connected to the recent past to want to put it all aside as though it were just a passing discomfort. He needed a little time to make sure that he had strength enough for the maximum effort.

He met with Anna and Carl for the first time since Max's funeral, in his old study. The dark rough-hewn paneling and subdued lighting seemed appropriate for a matter-of-fact discussion of what he was thinking about the party, his future with it, and their own involvement. They had both told him that they wanted to become more active in the party, but that it could only happen if he remained in a leadership role. He told them a little of his meeting with President, the walk in the Mall, and a hint of the anguishing reevaluation of his life that he had been experiencing. Neither of them so far felt reassured about his continuing tenure.

"I've done a lot of thinking about the great progress the party has made," he told them, " but I have to say that a lot of it's been sidetracked for me by what's happened. I still have a lot to think through, but right now I can say for sure that I want to go on as leader of the Reform Party. You know, even if I take on myself full blame for the deaths of Lyn and Max, it won't change anything. Right now I think that I would be honoring them more by continuing with the party work rather than dropping out. I know it's going to be hard, though, and I hope you will both stay by me as long as you can. You know, my world all seemed to fall apart when Lyn was killed, and then with Max . . ."

Anna stood next to Ed and put her arm around him. She was too emotional to say anything, but she knew by the way he gripped her arm that he knew she was with him all the way. Carl also put his hand on Ed's arm and said, "Dad, of course we'll be here. I think both Anna and I were thinking of leaving Woodville and starting lives somewhere else, but all that can wait. I've never felt that I had much of a direction in life, and I don't know anything about politics, but I do think that working for the party might actually be just what I've looked for. I know that Mora feels the same way. We both know that there's plenty of time for us to get into something else later, but who knows, maybe politics will be a career for us."

Ed turned to Anna, and asked, "How would Eric feel about your staying around to do party work?"

Anna smiled. "You'd have to ask him, but I'd say that this is just the sort of thing he would like to do. You know he's been doing freelance political writing for quite a while. I think he could really help shape up the party line."

Ed smiled and said, "You know how ironic it is that it took something truly traumatic to bring us together like this. It was also a lot of my fault, I know, but I never thought I knew you two very well before. I can't tell you how moving it is to feel we're part of a close family once more. Anna, you and Max took off when you were so young, and Carl, I never did know exactly how you spent your time."

Carl laughed, "I suppose you remember all those years when I used to go off by myself for hours."

"Of course I do. You know, I never did understand what you used to do on those long walks of yours. I know you snapped some pictures now and then, but there must have been more to it than that."

Carl laughed. "Yes, it must have seemed pretty odd for a workaholic like you to have a son idling away the days like that. Maybe it would be called obsessive-compulsive, but I found some of my best thoughts came during those times. It was almost like I was meditating in some kind of religion of my own, almost as though I could see into the infinite. I know it sounds silly, now."

"No, not silly. I just have trouble understanding it. I've taken a lot of walks, but I didn't react to them that way."

"Let's all go for a walk ourselves in the morning. Maybe I can explain."

Chapter 26
Botany

Ed and Carl met early in the breakfast room where they made coffee and snacked on leftovers. They decided to go on their walk together, leaving the others asleep or to whatever they may be doing. The day was a little gloomy, with an overcast muting the brightness of the sun, though it had risen early enough to warm the air comfortably by the time they reached the Zone. They walked together silently. Neither could seem to muster the small talk that could ease an awkward time like this. Carl began to wonder if he had made a mistake in bringing Ed out here, and especially in thinking he could somehow diminish his father's personal pain by talking to him about his own protracted meditations in this dilapidated neighborhood.

Carl had brought his camera and when their silence had become almost unbearable to him he took it out and began fiddling with the settings. Ed watched him, and finally said, "I always liked those pictures you made, Carl. I used to keep one in my little office when I was still trying to do research."

"I didn't know that. I did get some compliments from various people, mostly in the family, but I never knew you liked any of them that well. I always thought you would go more for modernistic things."

"No, I like these places, too. When I was just a kid, my father worked for a place that made oil tanks by riveting pieces together. There was rusting junk lying all around and I loved to wander through it. There's something about how temporary most things are that seems fascinating, at least it was for me. This place is like that, with the buildings falling apart and the plaster crumbling. You seem to feel the same way."

Carl said, "Yeah, I've spent, or maybe you'd say wasted, a lot of time thinking about all those people who so carefully put the paint or the plaster on years before, and how they were paid for it, and maybe even praised for doing such a good job. Then decades later it all comes off or falls apart. Other people can come along and stave off the decay for a while, but eventually it all seems to fall apart or get torn down. I've always thought the signs of decay can be really beautiful, not that different from looking at an old master painting and contemplating the long-dead artist who did it."

"Well, you're not alone in thinking that. Just go to some Italian cities that have reached a level of decay that can only be called perfectly beautiful. Venice and a hundred other cities are like that. It's too bad we humans can't age a little more like that, instead of just getting older and uglier and finally dying as helpless hulks, like these old buildings here."

"Is that the way you feel now?"

Ed's eyes rolled up a bit, as though this was a moment he did not relish. "I'm not quite there yet, but, you know, the terrible things that happened to our family have really made me feel old and sometimes nearly useless. For a while, I just didn't think I could go on. I'm feeling better now, but I have a way to go."

Carl said, "When I first started coming out here, I was pretty young, so I didn't spend much time thinking about death, especially my own. Later things that happened, like getting into the SOS and eventually seeing Mora nearly killed, changed all that. I knew it was inevitable that we get old and die, and suffer a lot of agonies in between, as well as pleasures. But it wasn't just thinking about the decaying buildings and how they sometimes get propped up to keep them going that made me feel better about dying. It was the weeds."

"The weeds?" Ed wasn't sure where the conversation was going.

"I took a lot of pictures of weeds too, you know. Nobody paid much attention to them, not nearly as much as to the shots of the light and dark walls of crumbling buildings. But the weeds kept me thinking for years. I even learned some of their names. People who have gardens seem to carry on a nonstop war with weeds, because they come up on their own year after year in spite of everything. They'll buy a plant, bring it home, and go through a lot of trouble to keep it alive, with special watering schedules, plant food, shade, all that. Even then they often die. Weeds are not like that."

Carl continued, "Just look down here by your feet. Along this crack the same weeds have been growing for years. They get killed back a bit in winter, but always come back. They have mastered an art of survival that seems almost eternal. I looked at them and felt I wanted to be like that – passive, keeping a low profile, but surviving and doing pretty well at it. I don't think I've been very successful, but the thought of the weeds kept me focused. I hate to say it, but without that focus I might have done what Max did. When I got into the Soldiers of Sacrifice I felt I just like those weeds. I hadn't done much of anything but here I was becoming something, surviving. Meeting Mora changed me completely. I don't pay much attention to the weeds anymore, but I've never forgotten the hours I spent here."

Ed felt uncomfortable with Carl's confession. He couldn't shake the idea that what Carl had told him was beginning to sound more than a little silly. After an awkwardly long pause, Carl said, "Well, Dad, I'll go back to check on Mora."

"Yes, you go on. I'll sit here for a while. I'm glad you're going to stay around to help out with the party work. We've got good people working here, but it's a comfort to me to have some family around, especially after what's happened lately."

Ed was alone for some time, making an effort to make sense of what Carl had said. He was startled when Anna approached him quietly and spoke.

"Hello, Dad. Carl told me you were here. I'm glad you talked with him."

"Yes, me too," Ed said. "I had no idea what he did out here."

"What do you think of his ideas?"

Ed replied, "I've been trying to understand him, but some of what he said, especially about the weeds. . . well, if you must know, I think it's mostly just crap. He seems to have made weeds some kind of a metaphor for survival, but there are a lot of really bad weeds, just like people. What's so great about their survival?   I wonder if he's serious."

"I think he's very serious," Anna said. "I don't know any more about his inner thoughts than you do, but whatever he's been doing all these years seems to have given him some strength."

"Yes, I suppose I'd feel better if I spent more time sitting out here and thinking things over. It's at least a good place for that. Actually, after Carl left, I did think about my own future, especially how I will relate to the party and where it may go."

Anna felt a little awkward after Ed's abrupt dismissal of what had been such a large part of Carl's life. Still, she wanted more than anything to be part of the new party, to give some meaning to her own life, so she had no intention of confronting Ed about much of anything at this point. Instead, she merely remarked, "Well, I think Carl is pretty serious about all this, but we don't all have to think the same way. What are your thoughts on the party now?"

"For one thing it's too narrow. I thought all we'd need is provide an outlet for the frustration of people being screwed by disasters, but now I know it has to do better than that. Maybe it is these damn weeds or the decrepit buildings that got to me, but it's really hit me that if we don't protect this world we live on, instead of just individual disasters that need attention the whole human population will spiral into one huge disaster. It's already happening, so we've got to have millions of people working like crazy all around the world to turn things around. I'm not smart enough by myself to do it, but maybe the Reform Party can start. We certainly can't rely on those idiots in Washington and Wall Street."

Anna said, "Don't you think it's tackling too much right now? Going after one big platform item at a time might be enough."

"I was just thinking of those global problems, and how social reform isn't much good if you don't have a decent world to live in." He paused for a while.

"There's always more that can be done I've been thinking about integrating environmental issues into the platform. Maybe Carl's right in one respect. He seems to be able to see something of the big picture by looking in a microscopic. I don't think it would hurt us to put some other serious proposals into our platform. There's no doubt that we will have to take all our energy from the sun, either water, wind, or solar, and forget everything else. While I was sitting here I estimated that if we covered an area of Nevada desert thirty miles square with solar cells, it would produce all the energy the country needs. With high temperature superconductors, it's easy to pump electricity all over the country to produce hydrogen in every town and city, for fuel cells, to run trains, to power the country. The land is sitting right there, with most of Nevada already owned by the government. What the hell are we waiting for?"

Ed took on a little of his old ranting self. Suddenly, he slumped, became silent and finally got up to walk back to the house. "But why do I ever think it could happen. The chiseling little politicians who make money from everything staying just the way it is, they'd find a way to block it. It probably is taking on too much anyway. The country isn't ready." His voice trailed off.

Anna said, "Dad, isn't that just what the Reform Party is all about – dumping the politicians and business people who are wrecking the country? You go on back. I'll stay here just a little while longer."

Ed's remarks had made her feel momentarily confused about how her future actions should be planned. Ed's dropping out of the party now was simply not an option she could imagine. As she sat on a large limestone block she thought of when the family was together, and Carl sat here alone. She tried to understand what he had found here, and came no closer than Ed had. Eventually she stood up, mentally shrugged off those thoughts, and walked back toward the house. She knew she had to get Ed back on track and throw herself into the looming political battle. She still had some doubts about Carl, but she knew that she could handle whatever came, and she'd be damn good at it.